"Trouble sleeping?" Alec's voice was a low rumble as he sauntered up beside her.

"Oh." Zoey turned, her heart thumping hard in her chest. "You startled me."

"You're not accustomed to having someone around."

"I guess I'm not." She dropped her gaze to the snow collecting on the fence post. Alec had a way of looking at her that made her feel exposed, and standing beside him in the darkness only exacerbated that sensation.

"Sorry," he murmured.

"Don't be." She cleared her throat and forced herself to look him in the eyes. Why was she suddenly so flustered? "I just got distracted."

He nodded toward the reindeer. "I can't blame you. They make a pretty picture at night."

"Gorgeous." She glanced again at the snowy scene. It was as if she and Alec had stepped straight into a Christmas movie. Visions of mistletoe danced in Zoey's head and she suddenly felt flushed, despite the cold.

"You okay?" Alec gave her a sideways glance.

"Sure. Why wouldn't I be?" Zoey shrugged, feigning nonchalance.

Mistletoe? Clearly, the reindeer weren't the only distraction on this ranch.

Books by Teri Wilson

Love Inspired

Alaskan Hearts
Alaskan Hero
Sleigh Bell Sweethearts

TERI WILSON

grew up as an only child and could often be found with her head in a book, lost in a world of heroes, heroines and exotic places. As an adult, her love of books has led her to her dream career—writing. Now an award-winning author of inspirational romance, Teri spends as much time as she can seeing exotic places for herself, then coming home and writing about them, of course. When she isn't traveling or spending quality time with her laptop, she enjoys baking cupcakes, going to movies and hanging out with her family, friends and five dogs. Teri lives in San Antonio, Texas, and loves to hear from readers. She can be contacted via her website at www.teriwilson.net.

Sleigh Bell Sweethearts

Teri Wilson

Recycling programs for this product may not exist in your area.

ISBN-13: 978-0-373-87851-2

SLEIGH BELL SWEETHEARTS

This edition published by arrangement with Love Inspired Books.

www.Harlequin.com

Printed in U.S.A.

Every good and perfect gift is from above,
coming down from the Father of heavenly lights….

—*James* 1:17

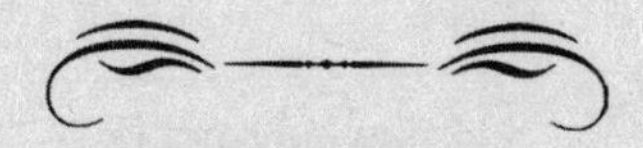

In loving memory of my father,
Robert K. Wilson, Jr.
Like Zoey, the heroine of this book,
in many ways I am my father's daughter.

Acknowledgments

I owe a huge debt of gratitude to Denise Hardy of Williams Reindeer Farm in Palmer, Alaska, for answering my many questions and doing her best to make a reindeer expert out of this Texas girl. Any and all reindeer errors are purely my own.

Many thanks to Elizabeth Winick and her staff at McIntosh & Otis. You are a dear friend, in addition to the best agent in the world!

And Rachel Burkot, my beloved editor—here's to our third book together! I hope there are many, many more.

Thank you to Meg Benjamin, my friend and valuable critique partner, for whipping this manuscript into shape.

Thank you to my family for always supporting me.

And as always, I thank God for making my dreams come true and allowing me to write for a living.

Chapter One

In her wildest dreams, Zoey Hathaway never thought she'd wind up an heiress. And dreaming was something of a specialty for Zoey. She'd been dreaming for the better part of her life.

But this...

She glanced overhead at the snow-covered arched sign that read Up on the Rooftop Reindeer Farm, wondering how in the world she'd lived in Aurora, Alaska, her entire life and never known such a place was nestled right in the cleft of the mountains. She'd never even heard of the place. And now, according to the lawyer who'd called her the day before, it was *her* reindeer farm.

...impossible.

"Smile!" Anya Parker, Zoey's friend and former boss, snapped a photo with her cell phone. "I still can't believe it. You're a reindeer heiress."

"I know. I'm having trouble processing it myself." Zoey peered at the snow-covered horizon, searching for a glimpse of antlers.

Nothing.

From what the lawyer had told her, this was a small operation. A hobby ranch—that was what he'd called it. Which made sense, considering she'd never even known Gus lived on a reindeer farm. Her flight instructor had been like a surrogate grandfather to her, but he'd been a man of few words. Too few, apparently.

She wondered where the reindeer were hiding. And how many of them were lurking around. Four? Six? A dozen? A dozen seemed like a lot. She was hoping for six, at most—a manageable handful. What could she possibly do with twelve or more reindeer?

"Gus really never told you about this place?" Anya asked.

"No." Zoey shook her head. "Over two hundred fifty hours of flight time and more ice-cream sundaes than I can count, and he never said a word. I always knew he lived alone, but he never mentioned the reindeer."

"No family," Anya whispered, her words dancing in the air in a fog of vapor. "How sad."

A lump formed in Zoey's throat.

Get a grip.

She swallowed it down. She'd never been one to feel sorry for herself, to bemoan the tragic circumstances life had thrown her way. And she wasn't about to start now. But picturing Gus living here alone—*dying* alone—was sobering, to say the least. She'd lost her parents when she was sixteen years old. And she hadn't seen her only other living relatives—an aunt and uncle who lived in the Lower 48—since the funeral. Zoey was every bit alone as Gus had been.

Will this happen to me someday?

Anya's arm slipped around her shoulders. "Poor choice of words. I'm sorry."

Zoey pasted on a smile. "It's okay."

"You're not alone. You know that, right?" Anya's eyebrows lifted. "I don't know a soul in Aurora who doesn't think of you as a little sister. You're the town sweetheart."

Zoey pulled a face. "I don't know about that."

Town sweetheart? That was awfully flattering. Too flattering, perhaps. Granted, Aurora had a way of taking care of its own. And Zoey had always felt cared for, even after she'd found herself adrift. But being known as the perennial kid sister had its downside, particularly in the romance department.

Town sweetheart? Town mascot was more like it.

Not that it mattered. When it came to men, Zoey had a way of making sure things never got too out of control. Sure, she'd dated. Some. But never the same guy more than a handful of times. Relationships led to attachment. And in her experience, attachment eventually led to loss and pain. She'd been down that road before.

No, thank you.

"And now that you're an heiress, who knows?" Anya gave her a playful hip bump. "Half a dozen marriage proposals will probably come your way by lunchtime."

Before Zoey could utter a word of protest—and she had plenty of them at the ready—a rumbling noise came at her out of nowhere. Beneath her feet, the snowy ground quaked. If she hadn't known better, she would have thought an avalanche was tumbling down the mountainside. But Anya's face showed no signs of alarm. And as a member of Aurora's Ski Patrol, Anya was something of an expert on avalanches, so Zoey exhaled a relieved, albeit curious, sigh.

"What is that?" Anya frowned as a cloud of snow on wheels came barreling toward them.

Zoey hopped backward out of its path, yet still managed to be on the receiving end of an onslaught of fine white powder. A chill ran through her as tiny pinpricks of cold sprayed her cheeks.

"Hey," she squealed.

The rumbling noise came to an abrupt stop.

Zoey blinked cold eyelashes against the sudden stillness. The white dust settled, revealing a rider clothed head to toe in black sitting astride a motorcycle. A large, powerful-looking motorcycle. Also black.

He parked directly beneath the reindeer farm's arched sign. At least she assumed it was a he. The rider's gender was impossible to discern, given all the protective gear—glossy helmet with an impenetrable jet-black face shield, sleek slim-fit parka and black leather gloves that covered not only his hands and wrists, but half his arms. Not a fraction of skin was visible.

Still, the thought of riding around on that thing sent a shiver up Zoey's spine.

A motorcycle?

In Alaska?

In December?

Man or woman, clearly the rider was insane. Insane and possibly suffering from frostbite.

Zoey cleared her throat as she took in the rider's broad shoulders and powerful build. Male. Most definitely. "Can I help you?"

The masked man swiveled his head in her direction.

Masked man? Really, Zoey...get a grip. He's not a superhero. Although all the black reminded her vaguely of Batman.

The Dark Knight lifted the helmet from his head. A fleece neck gaiter—black, of course—was pulled up over his mouth and nose, revealing nothing but a pair of frosty gray-blue eyes set below a head full of wildly disheveled dark hair.

He didn't look at all familiar. First the reindeer, and now a dangerous-looking biker. What else had Gus been hiding up here?

"I said, can I help you?" Zoey repeated, squaring her shoulders in an attempt to look authoritative. This was her reindeer farm, after all, even though she'd yet to lay eyes on a single antler.

Mystery Man gave Zoey a cursory once-over before pulling down the gaiter and exposing the rest of his face—high, sculpted cheekbones, an ultrastraight nose and a square jaw so firmly set that he looked as though he made a regular practice of grinding coal into diamonds with his teeth.

His gaze flitted to Anya briefly and settled once again on Zoey. "That depends."

"Depends?" She unzipped her parka a smidgen. Her neck was growing warm for some strange reason. "Depends on what?"

"You're not the new owner of this place, are you?" He lifted a single, threatening eyebrow.

She lifted her chin. "As a matter of fact, I am."

"Well, it's about time," he seethed.

Zoey's mouth dropped open. Who was this guy? "Excuse me?"

"Perhaps introductions are in order." Anya stepped between them.

Zoey sent up a silent prayer of thanks for Anya's presence. Facing the irritable Man in Black wasn't exactly something she would have liked to do alone. Not that she was afraid of him. She'd certainly faced more frightening things than a biker in the wilds of Alaska. He was just a bit intense. And she still had no clue what he was doing on *her* reindeer farm, acting as if he owned the place.

Anya thrust a mittened hand at him. "I'm Anya Parker, and this is Zoey Hathaway. And you are?"

He pulled off one of his gloves and shook Anya's hand. "Alec Wynn."

His gazed shifted back to Zoey. She reached for his hand and shook it. It was surprisingly warm given his chosen method of transportation.

"Hi, Alec," she said, offering him a polite smile. Perhaps they'd simply gotten off on the wrong foot.

He smiled right back at her. Even his smile possessed an edge. "You owe me a thousand dollars."

Um...what?

She blinked. Once. Twice. Three times.

Alec's smile faded as he crossed his arms and leaned back on the seat of his bike, apparently waiting for her to say something. Or whip out her checkbook.

Zoey's throat grew thick. "Perhaps there's been a misunderstanding..."

"Nope. No misunderstanding." He shook his head. "This is your reindeer farm, is it not?"

"Well..." She glanced at Anya, who could do nothing but shrug, then back at Alec. Zoey still had no clue who he actually was, other than a purported creditor. "...yes. But I've only owned it for a day. Less than twenty-four hours, actually."

She couldn't possibly owe him a thousand dollars. For starters, she didn't have that kind of money.

Technically, she did, she supposed. But that money was part of the down payment for the airplane she was buying in five days. The airplane that was to be the start of her new career as a professional pilot. She'd worked eight years as a barista, scrimping and saving for that down payment. It took a lot of lattes to buy a plane, even a small one.

Her plane money was off-limits. She'd already given notice at the coffee bar. Next Monday was to be her first official day as a charter pilot, and she couldn't very well fly without an airplane.

Alec's gaze narrowed. He was looking less and less like a superhero with each passing second. "Twenty-four hours?"

"Thereabouts." She glanced at Anya again, eliciting a hearty nod of agreement.

"Maybe you could provide Zoey with some background information," Anya said.

"Yes. Background information would be delightful," Zoey muttered under her breath.

At least she'd thought it was under her breath. The storm clouds gathering in Alec's eyes told her differently. "As I said before, my name is Alec Wynn. I work here. For you, apparently."

So she'd inherited both a reindeer farm and a surly man on a Harley. Perfect. "How odd."

"Odd?" He angled his head, and a lock of unruly hair fell across his forehead.

Why am I looking at his hair? Surely that violated some sort of employer/employee boundary line. But how would she know? She'd never been anyone's boss before. "Yes. I mean, what exactly do you do for Gus? I mean, me."

This was beyond surreal. If her nose wasn't so cold, she'd wonder if she were dreaming.

"I care for the reindeer," he said, as if it was the most obvious thing in the world. "And generally keep things running around here."

"Aurora's a small town. I've never laid eyes on you before. Where have you been hiding yourself?"

"I've only worked here a week. I spent my first day on the job giving my employer CPR. Unsuccessfully." Alec's gaze dropped to his hands. He paused a beat before continuing. "And now I've been feeding a herd of reindeer—*on my dime*—while I wait around to see what's to become of this place. So, forgive me if I haven't had time to make the social rounds."

Oh.

Oh...

So Alec had been the one to find Gus. This was new information. And it softened Zoey toward him a bit, even though she still thought him awfully demanding. And difficult. Couldn't he have mentioned this right off the bat? "I'm sorry."

He looked back up. Some of the tension had left his eyes, leaving a hint of pain in its place. "I'm sorry, too. For your loss. Are you his daughter?"

"Oh, no. I'm not family. Gus was my flight instructor." She swallowed. "And my friend."

His brow furrowed. "I see." Clearly, he didn't.

Which was fine. Zoey didn't really understand it herself.

"So, this thousand dollars," Anya said, directing them back to the matter at hand. "Is it your salary?"

Surely not. A thousand dollars a week? To feed a couple of reindeer? Although performing CPR was probably above and beyond the call of duty.

"No. Gus paid me a month up front because I moved here from Washington to take the job."

For the first time, Zoey noticed the Washington State license plate on the motorcycle. She wondered if he'd actually ridden the thing all the way up through snow-covered Canada. It didn't seem feasible.

Alec continued. "I'm out a fair bit now for reindeer food, hay and other incidentals. I can provide receipts."

A fair bit. *Lord, please don't let it be even* more *than a thousand dollars*. "How much do they eat? A thousand dollars is a lot of money."

He shrugged. "You've got a lot of reindeer."

Zoey grew very still. The snowflakes swirling around them seemed to move in slow motion. "I do?"

At long last, Alec Wynn smiled—a slight lift of one corner of his lips. It was the subtlest of gestures, but just lethal enough to uncurl a ribbon of dread in Zoey's belly. "Yes, ma'am. You certainly do."

* * *

Alec watched the color drain from Zoey's face. The pink in her wind-kissed complexion faded right before his eyes.

"How many, exactly?" she asked.

There was really no way to sugarcoat it. And anyway, Alec believed in telling things like they were. "Thirty."

"Thirty?" she echoed. She exchanged a glance with her friend—*Anya,* if Alec remembered correctly—who'd been watching their exchange with what appeared to be keen interest. *"Thirty!"*

"Give or take," he added.

Zoey's gaze narrowed. She had lovely eyes. If Alec had been the romantic sort—and he most definitely was *not*—they probably would have reminded him of the moss-covered Sitka spruce trees that shaded the Olympic Forest back in Washington. "You mean, you don't know?"

"Of course I know." He lifted an irritated brow. "It's thirty. Usually. Palmer, one of the boys, keeps escaping. When he decides to grace us with his presence, it's thirty-one."

Anya snickered, failing in her obvious attempt not to laugh. "Zoey, you've inherited a rogue reindeer."

Zoey's mouth fell open. "This really isn't funny. What am I supposed to do with thirty-sometimes-thirty-one reindeer?"

Alec felt as if he should comfort her or something, which was ludicrous. What was he supposed to say? *Sorry about your charmed life, sweetheart.*

She looked as though she might faint dead away. He really hoped she didn't. His last attempts to revive someone hadn't worked out so well. Then again, that shouldn't have come as a shock. Sometimes it seemed as if everything he touched turned to ruin. Why should Alaska be any different?

All he'd wanted was a fresh start. He'd been looking for a new beginning all his life. Was that really too much to ask?

Apparently so.

He'd driven his bike more than two thousand miles in four days to get here, only to find himself holding the lifeless body of Gus Henderson within a day of his arrival.

He balled his hands into fists and pounded them against his thighs in an effort to shake off the memory. As bad as things in his life had been—and they'd been plenty bad—he'd never held a dying man in his arms before. It wasn't an event he cared to repeat. Ever.

"Zoey, take a deep breath. Everything is going to be fine." Anya wrapped an arm around Zoey's shoulders. "Why don't I call the lawyer and see if we can get to the bottom of this?"

Zoey gave a robotic nod. "That sounds good. Thank you."

"His number is on the paper work in the car. I'll go give him a call. Alec, it was nice meeting you. Welcome to Alaska." Anya waved at him and headed toward the SUV parked on the edge of the street.

Relief, mixed with a healthy dose of annoyance, had washed over Alec when he'd first spotted the unfamiliar vehicle. The new owner had shown up. *Finally.* For nearly a week, he'd been muddling his way through things until someone who knew what they were doing decided to join him.

Alec glanced at Zoey Hathaway standing beside him. Clearly, she didn't know the first thing about reindeer. He couldn't help but wonder about her relationship with Gus. Judging by the shock etched on her delicate features, she'd never set foot on the ranch before. It should have seemed strange for a student to inherit her flight instructor's property like this. Should have, but didn't. Not really. Zoey seemed exactly like the sort of person who skipped through life as though it were a cakewalk.

She was pretty. Long, silky blond hair…and those luminous green eyes. Even out here where the temperature dipped below twenty degrees, she was perfectly put together. She wore fur-trimmed boots, black leggings and a cheery red parka. Her winter hat was also red, decorated with—irony of ironies—prancing reindeer.

Everything about her was sweet. Too sweet. Like the Easter Bunny, the Tooth Fairy and Santa Claus all rolled into one perky package.

And now she was his boss.

The very idea gave him a headache.

It wasn't a cruel enough twist of fate that he'd ended up on a reindeer farm? Four weeks before Christmas? The ad he'd answered on Craigslist for a ranch hand never mentioned reindeer. Granted, the work was in Alaska. But he'd expected horses. Or elk. Not Rudolph.

How did a boy who'd never had a Christmas tree, never sat on Santa's knee, grow into a man who lived on a reindeer farm in Alaska?

He pushed the thought away. He was here now, so he might as well deal with it. He wasn't going anywhere. Not without the money he was owed. "Shall I show you?"

Zoey snapped out of her daze and blinked up at him. "The reindeer?"

"Yes. Would you like to see them?"

She nodded. "Very much."

With a flick of his wrist, he cranked the motorcycle to life. "Hop on."

"On that thing?" She frowned at the bike.

"We're driving all of fifty feet. You're not scared, are you?" He offered her his helmet.

She jerked it out of his hand. "Please. Of course not."

He watched her as she removed her hat and replaced it with the helmet. It was far too big. Alec did his best to suppress his amused grin. Something told him now was definitely not the time to laugh at her.

He scooted forward on the seat of the bike, making room for her behind him. Zoey swung her leg over and situated herself on the seat. Alec waited for her to clasp her arms around his waist or, at the very least, grab hold of his parka.

Nothing happened.

He glanced over his shoulder. "You might want to hang on. You can wrap your arms around me. I won't bite."

He couldn't see a thing through the face shield of the helmet, but he would have bet she was rolling her eyes.

"I've known you all of five minutes," she said.

"Suit yourself." He released the clutch, and the tires rolled and crunched over the snow.

Alec did his best to make the ride a smooth one. Tossing his new boss out of her seat didn't seem like a smart thing to do, even though she would have had it coming. Apparently, she was every bit as stubborn as she was cute. *Great.*

Despite the fact that Alec had cleared the path with a snowblower an hour or so ago, it was a bit bumpy. Just as they made their way around the log cabin, which stood at the front of the property, the bike hit a slippery groove in the hard-packed snow. The motorcycle lurched to the right. Alec corrected the steering before Zoey could take a tumble, but immediately afterward he felt her arms wrap around his waist.

I told you so, his thoughts screamed. Even so, having her arms around him wasn't altogether unpleasant.

She held on tight until they reached the fence and Alec cut the engine. Then she hopped off. With record-breaking swiftness.

"You didn't ride all the way here from Washington on this thing, did you?" she asked as she removed the helmet.

He took it from her and hung it on the handlebars. "How else do you think it got here?"

"It sounds a little dangerous. Not to mention cold." She made an attempt to smooth her hair. It wasn't all that successful.

For some reason, the sight of her—cheeks pink, perfect blond hair slightly mussed—made him smile. "You don't like motorcycles?"

"I didn't say that." She didn't have to. "It just doesn't seem like the most practical method of transportation this close to the arctic circle. But suit yourself."

Oh, I will. He didn't need her permission to drive his motorcycle. He could ride around in a flying saucer if he wanted. She might be his boss, but she wasn't his mother.

Not that his mother had ever cared a whit about him. She'd been too busy getting high and avoiding the angry swings of his father to pay much attention to him.

He stalked toward the fence without saying a word. Zoey crunched through the snow behind him.

The Chugach mountain range rose before them in jagged silver peaks. Low-hanging clouds obscured the mountaintops, and a layer of what looked like fog spread out over the base of the foothills. Then the fog rolled toward them. A spectacular set of antlers came into view. Then another, and another.

Dozens of reindeer trotted toward them, kicking up snow so thick that their legs were barely visible. They appeared to float in a snowy mist, as though carried by a cloud of glittering ice crystals.

"Oh, my," Zoey whispered.

Alec recognized the wonder in her tone. He'd felt the same way the first time he'd seen the reindeer. As much as he hated to admit it, the sight of them still sometimes took his breath away. Even if the whole thing was a little too Norman Rockwell for his taste.

"Beautiful, aren't they?" he asked, his throat growing tight.

"They sure are." Her green eyes sparkled. "Are they always so quiet? I feel as if I'm looking at a dream…something that's not quite real."

He took a sidelong glance at Zoey and felt a wholly unexpected flicker of connection with her. "They typically don't make much noise. I think they like the cold. They seem happy to run and play most of the time."

Then she opened her mouth, and the moment was gone. "You mean play reindeer games?"

She just had to go there—the saccharine-sweet Christmas route. He really should have expected it.

With great reluctance, Alec said, "I suppose you could call it that."

She laughed, oblivious to the mercurial change in his mood. "I just had no idea. Gus never told me about any of this."

And yet the man had given it to her. All of it. "I suppose this sort of thing happens to you all the time."

She frowned but somehow managed to look all wide-eyed and innocent. "What sort of thing?"

"Inheriting reindeer farms and the like." He hadn't meant to inject acid into his tone, but there it was all the same.

"Actually, no. It doesn't." Zoey's eyes flashed. Alec was thrown for a minute by the fire in her gaze. Fire aimed directly at him. "If you think I'm some sort of spoiled princess, Mr. Wynn, you're sorely mistaken. I suppose I can't really blame you. Usually people who inherit things—houses, money, *reindeer*—come from privilege. Or at least from loving homes. I have neither of those things. So you might want to revisit your first impression of me. I'm not your average heiress."

She spun on her heel and stomped back down the path toward the waiting SUV, leaving Alec to wonder what had just transpired.

Zoey Hathaway had surprised him. And people didn't surprise him often. In fact, he couldn't remember the last time anyone had.

Zoey Hathaway...average?

Hardly.

Chapter Two

"*North Pole Nails?* Really?" Zoey glanced at the sign on the door of the nail salon where Anya and their mutual friend Clementine had suggested they meet for an emergency pedicure session. "I thought the purpose of this mission was to make me forget about reindeer."

Anya opened the door and nudged Zoey inside. "That's our intention. I promise. But it's not like Aurora is teeming with day-spa options."

"Try to pretend it's called something else, something non-Christmasy," Clemetine said.

Try *not* to think about Christmas? When it was less than a month away? That idea only made Zoey feel worse. "I love Christmas. I just never imagined I'd be spending it with my very own herd of reindeer."

Or that they were such expensive creatures.

She would have been perfectly happy to stop thinking about her reindeer's spending habits. But that wasn't possible. She'd even declined the pedicure offer at first. Surely she had something else she should be spending her money on. Like reindeer chow or something.

What do they eat, anyway? I don't even know.

She really shouldn't be here. This afternoon was one of her

regularly scheduled volunteer shifts at the church thrift store. Staffed entirely by volunteers, the thrift shop raised money to help a few of the impoverished, hard-to-reach communities out in the bush, the area of Alaska that was inaccessible by roads. Having flown with Gus on numerous missions of mercy to such villages, Zoey had a heart for the people of the bush. But her pressing need to see her lawyer had thrown a wrench into her afternoon plans.

Since when had she become the sort of person who met with lawyers?

Since she became an heiress.

One thing had become crystal clear over the course of the morning—being an heiress wasn't all that it was cracked up to be.

"Sit down and take off your shoes. And smile. This is supposed to be fun. Remember?" Anya steered Zoey by her shoulders to one of the sumptuous leather spa chairs.

Zoey sank into it, and Anya flipped a switch. The chair hummed to life. "What's that noise?"

"It's a massage chair. Relax. Please." Anya sank into the next chair.

"Are you sure your mom is okay with this?" Zoey frowned. Anya's mother headed up the church thrift store. As a seamstress, it was pretty much her baby.

"She's fine. I just talked to her. She's got more volunteers there this afternoon than she has customers. The thrift store is fine. Everything and everyone is fine, except for you, apparently." Anya pointed at Zoey's feet.

She took the hint. She removed her snow boots, dipped her bare feet in the tub of warm, bubbly water in front of her chair and said a prayer of thanks that her friends had insisted on treating her to this little luxury.

"Did you get a chance to meet with the lawyer yet?" Clementine asked as she settled into the chair immediately to Zoey's left.

"Yes. I just came from his office, actually." Zoey nodded and selected a color from the tiny bottles of polish the nail technician offered up for inspection.

Anya chose next—fire-engine red. "What did he say? Could he shed any light on the situation?"

"He apologized for misleading me into thinking there were only a few reindeer on Gus's property. Apparently, thirty is a modest number as far as reindeer are concerned." So was thirty-one. Zoey couldn't help but wonder where Palmer, the errant reindeer, was right now. Should she be concerned?

She hoped not. She had more than enough on her plate without having to worry about a defiant reindeer roaming the city streets.

"Really?" Clementine's eyes grew wide. "What's a large number, then?"

"A hundred or more." Zoey supposed she should be relieved. A hundred? She couldn't even imagine. Although if she couldn't afford thirty, what difference did it make? She might as well have inherited *five* hundred of them.

"Did he mention your mysterious employee?" Anya's lips curved into a smirk.

"There's an employee, too?" Clementine asked.

Anya's smile grew wider. "Oh, yes. His name is Alec, and he's rather handsome."

Handsome?

Zoey couldn't argue against that assessment, but she considered it far too tame an adjective to apply to Alec. She could think of a few words that fit, however—*dangerous, moody...tempting.*

"He's also borderline rude, so you can wipe that grin off your face." Zoey's cheeks grew warm. She blamed it on the bubbly footbath and the heated massage chair. "And I happen to owe him a thousand dollars."

Anya's smile morphed into a frown. "That was real?"

"Unfortunately, yes." Zoey had pretty much committed to memory the itemized list the lawyer had shown her—fencing supplies, food, hay, straw and yet more fencing supplies. Apparently Palmer's urge to escape ran deep. He wasn't about to let something as silly as a fence stand between him and his freedom.

Clementine reached over and gave her arm a squeeze. "What are you going to do?"

Zoey inhaled a deep breath. Could she even bring herself to utter the lawyer's suggestion aloud?

"I have a few options," she said cryptically.

Anya and Clementine exchanged confused glances.

"Such as?" Anya asked.

"There's a log cabin on the property. I thought I could move in there. With the money I save on rent, I might be able to reimburse Alec sometime this century."

"And then what?" Clementine said, leaning her head back against her comfy leather pedicure chair and closing her eyes.

Zoey stared down at her feet in the soapy water. She couldn't even look her friends in the eyes. How could she possibly go through with it? "There's a buyer who's interested in the herd."

"Really?" Clementine's eyes popped back open. "That sounds promising. Maybe you could keep a few—two or three, possibly—and sell the rest. Or do you think they'd miss one another? Do reindeer form attachments like that?"

How would Zoey know? She didn't know the first thing about the interpersonal relationships of reindeer. And she certainly couldn't afford a reindeer psychiatrist. "Missing their friends would be the least of their concerns."

Anya's gaze slid toward Zoey. "What aren't you telling us?"

Zoey inhaled a deep breath. She decided to just spit it out. “The prospective buyer is a commercial reindeer breeder.”

Clementine frowned as she appeared to turn Zoey’s words over in her head. “What does that mean, exactly?”

Anya, born and raised in Alaska like Zoey, knew precisely what it meant. “If a commercial breeder buys the herd, they’ll end up as reindeer hot dogs.”

Clementine winced. “Oh.”

“I don’t know if I can do it.” It wasn’t as if Zoey hadn’t eaten her share of reindeer hot dogs in her lifetime. In Alaska, they were practically as common as peanut butter and jelly. But these weren’t just any reindeer.

They were Gus’s reindeer.

Her inheritance.

She swallowed around the lump that had taken up residence in her throat since she’d first heard those impossible words from Gus’s lawyer: *you’re Mr. Henderson’s heir.*

The phone had nearly slipped out of her hand. She’d been sure she was hearing things. Or dreaming. Things like this didn’t happen in real life. At least, not to Zoey.

She’d been sixteen when her parents died in a small plane crash just north of the Chugach Mountains. It had been a freak accident, the product of a mountain downdraft. Her dad had been the pilot. Even when faced with the sudden loss of her family, the only thing she’d inherited had been her father’s love of flight. Aviation hadn’t simply been a livelihood for her dad. It had been his passion.

Zoey’s own fascination with flight had started on the very day of her parents’ funeral. She could pinpoint the moment exactly—she’d been sitting in the front pew of the Aurora Community Church, listening as one pilot after another eulogized her father, speaking of his passion for flying and the love he had for the extraordinary beauty of Alaska.

The last of them had been Gus. His words had struck up

a symphony of memories in Zoey—being buckled into the backseat of her dad's Super Cub, looking out the window at spouting whales and sandstone peaks or touching down at some pristine, unspoiled place. As she'd relived one moment after another, she felt closer to her parents. It had been almost as if they were still alive, even though their bodies rested in coffins nearly close enough for her to reach out and touch. After the memorial service, she'd gone home and collapsed on her childhood bed for the last time, and she'd imagined she was soaring through a cloudless winter sky.

It was the only thing that kept her from crying. When her aunt and uncle told her she was to go home with them to Kentucky and leave her beloved Alaska, she'd squeezed her eyes closed and thought about what it would be like to float above the mountains with her arms spread wide and the wind whipping through her hair. Her musings about flight became her refuge.

She knew better than to tell anyone, particularly her aunt and uncle. She was sure it would worry them, and she'd had enough trouble convincing them to let her stay in Aurora to finish out her last year and a half of high school. The members of the church, particularly the pastor and his family, took her in. They were the closest thing to family she had left in Alaska.

And still, she kept her daydreams of flight to herself. It was a secret between her and God. Without a doubt, people would find her sudden fascination with aviation worrisome. Or even morbid, perhaps. But to Zoey, it was her way of remaining her father's daughter in the days, weeks and years after his passing.

Her inheritance was a passion for the thing he loved most, the thing that ultimately took his life and that of Zoey's mother. But it was the only thing she had.

Until the reindeer.

"I don't want to sell them." Was it what Gus would have wanted? Zoey was sure it wasn't. But why did he have the reindeer in the first place? And why had he left them to her?

They'd been close. After hearing him speak at the funeral, Zoey had sought him out. Gus seemed to have known exactly what she wanted, because he told her more stories about her father. Things she'd never heard before. Stories that fed her soul in those dark days. Her unconventional friendship with Gus was rooted in mutual grief.

They'd begun meeting for ice cream once a week and kept up the habit even after all Gus's stories had been told three times over. She'd come to think of him as family. He'd always been there for her, whether she needed consoling when no one asked her to the senior homecoming dance or just needed to know how to change the oil in her car. Once, in a rare moment of sentimentality during one of their many flights together, he'd looked over at her and told her she was like the daughter he'd never had.

But it still wasn't the same thing. People just didn't leave things like reindeer farms to their friends. Even close ones.

Why me, Lord? "I want to keep them. All thirty-sometimes-thirty-one of them. Is that crazy?"

Anya propped her feet up, her toes ready and waiting for red polish. "Sort of."

"Sometimes thirty-one? Have you lost count of your reindeer already?" Clementine grinned.

"Trust me. You don't want to know." Zoey closed her eyes and did her best to forget about the reindeer farm.

She made little progress. Even when her foot massage got under way, she was still distracted by thoughts of reindeer chow, moving from her apartment into the cabin on the ranch and what would happen on Friday when she was supposed to deliver the check for the down payment on her airplane.

A Super Cub, just like her father's. She was so close to making her dreams come true. At last.

Perhaps Alec would be open to some sort of payment arrangement. Somehow, she doubted it. He'd been pretty blunt about asking for his money. And though she was loath to admit it, she found him a little intimidating. After her grand speech about how he'd misjudged her, she'd fled. *Fled!* As if all the reindeer weren't enough of a handful, she had Alec Wynn's brooding intensity to contend with.

From the depths of her purse, her cell phone rang. Alec's chiseled face flashed in her mind, although why she'd want to hear from him was a mystery.

She fished her ringing phone out of her purse with the intention of simply turning the ringer off. But when she saw all the missed-call notifications on the screen, she paused. "I have five missed calls."

Clementine looked up from the magazine in her lap. "Who from?"

"I'm not sure." Zoey answered the call before it rolled to voice mail again. "Hello?"

"Is this Zoey Hathaway?" It was a man. He sounded exasperated but polite, which ruled out Alec entirely.

"Yes." She was hyperaware of everyone's eyes on her. Clementine, Anya and even the manicurists were all watching her with mounting curiosity. "How can I help you?"

"This is Chuck Baker, out at the airfield."

Zoey bit her lip. Chuck was the head air-traffic-control officer at the town's one and only airport, located at the back of the Northern Lights Inn, the heart of Aurora. For years, she'd poured Chuck's coffee from behind the hotel's coffee bar. Double espresso in the morning. Decaf in the afternoon. And she'd spoken to him countless times from the cockpit once she'd started her flying lessons.

But he'd never called her before.

"Chuck, hi." Nerves bounced around in her stomach for reasons she couldn't quite pinpoint. "What's up?"

"It seems we've got a situation down here at the airport." The frustration in his tone kicked up a notch.

Zoey gripped the phone tighter. What if there'd been an accident? *Lord, please no. Not again.* Somewhere in the logical part of her brain, Zoey knew this wasn't the case. Why would Chuck call her, of all people, if there'd been a tragedy? "A situation? I hope no one is hurt."

"No one's hurt. It's nothing like that. But we've had to ground all flights. It's chaos down here, and if we don't get things under control you'll be facing a hefty fine from the FAA."

Hefty fine?

She blinked. What could she have possibly done to incur a fine? She was in the middle of a foot massage. What might the Federal Aviation Administration have against pedicures? "I don't understand. Have I done something wrong?"

"Not you, per se." He released a sigh. "It's your reindeer."

Zoey's panicked gaze darted up to Clementine and Anya. "My reindeer?"

"Yep. There's a big, fat reindeer parked in the middle of the runway. He won't budge, and rumor has it he's yours."

Palmer.

Oh, please, God. No.

Alec slid onto a barstool at the coffee counter at the Northern Lights Inn and fought the urge to drop his head into his hands. Exhaustion had worked its way deep into his bones. The past six days had been a killer. Not that he was complaining—he'd always relished the opportunity to lose himself in a hard day's work. There was a sweetness to forgetting…forgetting the past, the present, the future and living fully in the moment. And forgetting had never come easily to Alec.

Growing up in a home with parents who struggled with addiction had provided him with a laundry list of things he'd just as soon forget. At the best of times, his mom and dad had been too out of it to function. In the worst, there'd been the beatings—usually a product of sweaty, heated withdrawal from all the drugs. Alec had witnessed the angry cycle for seventeen years until he'd finally made the decision to leave home and never look back. The leaving had been easy. It was the looking back he sometimes still struggled with.

Since arriving in Alaska, he'd almost managed it. That was a good thing, since he'd traveled to the literal edge of the continent. If he couldn't outrun his past here, there was nowhere else to go without falling into the stormy waters of the Bering Sea.

Finding Gus Henderson sprawled facedown in the snow hadn't been the best of starts. It was a stark reminder to Alec that he could run all he wanted, but wherever he went, trouble would always be there to find him. Ironically, it was the reindeer that had kept him sane in the aftermath. He couldn't very well leave. Who would care for them?

"Can I get you something?" the barista asked.

Alec looked up. "Sure, thanks. Coffee. Black."

"Tough day?" The guy seated two barstools away glanced in Alec's direction. He had a red parka slung on the back of his chair and a copper-colored dog curled at his feet.

Alec noticed they both looked vaguely familiar. "You could say that."

Working for the forest service in Olympic State Park back in Washington had prepared him somewhat for the brutal weather, but he'd been completely inexperienced in the reindeer department. He'd gotten himself up to speed on the reindeer soon enough, but traveling north through Canada on his bike, the sudden death of his new employer and the daily demands of running the ranch solo were beginning to catch up with him.

And now there was the farm's new owner to contend with.

Alec couldn't help but wonder if she would prove to be far more trouble than she was worth.

"You new in town?" the stranger asked. "I don't think I've seen you around before."

"I just moved here a week ago." Alec accepted his coffee from the barista and took a long, hot swallow. It burned its way down his throat. "Alec Wynn. I'm working at a reindeer farm up in the hills about five miles from here. Nice dog, by the way."

"Thanks. Brock Parker." He offered his hand over the empty barstool between them. "Welcome."

"Thank you." Alec frowned. Brock looked familiar, and Alec was almost certain he'd heard the name before. Just what he didn't want, or need—a face from his past.

Brock appeared to study him for a moment. He took a sip of his own coffee and grinned. "I think you may have met my wife earlier today out at the reindeer farm."

Wife?

A wholly unexpected pang hit Alec in the chest. Could Zoey Hathaway be married?

Then he remembered the rather heart-wrenching look in those green eyes of hers when she'd unleashed her *I'm-not-your-average-heiress* outburst on him. She couldn't possibly have a husband. Not a decent kind of guy, anyway. A decent man wouldn't make her feel as if she hadn't come from a loving home, even if it were the case.

He swallowed. What did he know about decent guys? It wasn't as if he would ever be that kind of man, considering where he'd come from. He'd tried the decent route before—the Sunday-school, one-woman kind of route. He'd even gone so far as to put a ring on the woman's finger.

Marriage. He'd thought it was something he could do. Not like his parents, of course. Better. He'd reveled in the idea of doing it the right way—two people bound together by God.

He'd never gotten the chance. His fiancée's family had made sure of it. *The apple doesn't fall far from the tree,* they'd said.

She'd believed it. Why shouldn't Alec? He'd be lying if he said he'd never wrestled with the fear that he would one day end up like his parents.

He turned his attention once again to Brock. "Your wife?"

Brock nodded. "Her name is Anya."

Anya. The friend. Of course. "Yes, we met. Very nice lady."

"She and Zoey are good friends. I think they're out getting pedicures right now, actually." Brock shrugged. "They worked together for a while here at the coffee bar, before Anya started up full time with the ski patrol and Zoey decided to buy her airplane."

Alec's hand tightened around his coffee mug.

So Zoey Hathaway went around getting pedicures and buying airplanes...but she wasn't a spoiled princess.

Yeah, right.

And to think for a split second, he'd thought they might actually have something in common.

"Hey, speaking of Zoey..." Brock rose from his barstool and took a few steps toward the window overlooking the frozen lake behind the hotel. The dog scrambled to its feet and followed on Brock's heels. "Is that her?"

Alec took another swig of his coffee. He didn't bother looking out the window. Unless she was writing him a check, what Zoey did was none of his concern. "Hmm?" he muttered, more to have something to say rather than expressing any real interest in whatever was going on outside.

"That's her, all right." There was a hint of worry in Brock's tone that Alec did his best to ignore. "Is she trying to get herself killed?"

Now how was he supposed to ignore a question like that?

Alec dragged his reluctant gaze to the window. Sure enough, there was Zoey Hathaway—her blond princess hair tumbling out of her merry red hat and flying around in the wind as she tiptoed her way past a row of small airplanes, across the ice-covered lake.

Forget it. Forget her. It's not your business. "That's not the runway, is it?"

"I'm afraid it is," Brock said.

"What is she doing out there?" Alec slid off his barstool for a closer look. Not that he had any intention of rescuing her. He was curious. That was all.

Brock said nothing. He simply pointed.

As Alec followed the direction of Brock's finger, his gaze landed on a familiar antlered friend.

Palmer.

Chapter Three

Alec struggled to gain his footing on the slippery surface of the lake. He'd already slid his way to the middle of the runway, and Zoey was still a good ten feet ahead of him. She was shockingly fast. And agile.

"What do you think you're doing?" he shouted.

She turned her head and stopped in her tracks when she spotted him. "What are you doing here?"

"I asked first." He kept plodding toward her.

"If you must know, I'm trying to save myself a bucketful of money." She resumed her trek across the ice.

"Could you stop for *one minute?* Please," he all but growled.

Amazingly, she did.

By the time he reached her, he was struggling to catch his breath. She, on the other hand, was perfectly composed—waiting for him with her hands on her hips.

"How can I help you?" she asked, as if the situation was completely normal—as if standing in the center of an active airport runway, pausing for a moment from her pursuit of a petulant reindeer, was an everyday occurrence.

"This is crazy dangerous. You know that, right?" He glowered at her.

"You seem mad." She frowned. "Are you mad at me? I mean, about something other than the thousand dollars?"

Alec inhaled a ragged breath. The cold Alaskan air burned his lungs, making him long for the coffee he'd abandoned in order to take up this wild-goose chase. "This doesn't have anything to do with how I feel about you."

Her cheeks blazed almost as red as her hat.

"What I mean to say is that I've already had one boss die on me this week. Let's not make it two." He jammed a hand through his hair and noticed his fingers were already numb. In the rush to get out here and put an end to this madness, he'd forgone his hat and gloves. "I have no desire to see you splattered under the wheels of an airplane. What are you doing?"

She waved a dainty hand toward Palmer, who appeared blissfully unaware that he was in her cross hairs. "I'm removing my reindeer from the path of air traffic."

"By throwing yourself into the middle of that traffic?" He had to shout to make himself heard over a prop plane that had just fired up its engine. Great. They were probably both about to be chopped to bits by that propeller.

Why couldn't he have simply minded his own business? Zoey Hathaway could obviously take care of herself. He looked around at all the airplanes idling with puffs of white smoke trailing from their engines. One or two planes circled overhead, clearly ready to land. Okay, maybe not so obviously. But why did he have to be the one to make sure she didn't get hurt?

Alec shook his head. He had no answer for that particular question.

"Would you relax?" She rolled her eyes. They looked even greener out here, surrounded by the vast field of white. Irish green, one of the park rangers at Olympic Forest used to call it. Alec was sure he could see a whole spectrum of color in that one single hue. "The tower has grounded all flights, both outgoing and incoming. I'm not going to get 'splattered under the wheels of an airplane,' as you so eloquently put it."

"Really?" He lifted his brows.

"Really." She resumed her march toward Palmer, who was now lying down in the center of the runway with his long legs folded beneath him.

Oh, boy. Alec recognized the posture and knew Palmer had no intention of moving any time soon. Within minutes, the reindeer would probably be snoring loudly enough to rival the whir of the surrounding plane engines.

"That's good news," Alec said and fell in step beside her.

"No, it's not. It's not good news at all." She released a sigh, and a cloud of her breath danced in the air. "The FAA doesn't take kindly to interruptions in air traffic. I could be looking at a big fine."

Alec had a feeling he could kiss his thousand dollars goodbye, which made his presence out here all the more nonsensical. "I see."

"Wait a minute." Zoey came to a halt about twenty feet away from Palmer's resting spot. Her lips quirked into a smile.

Alec's gaze was drawn at once to her mouth. *She's even prettier when she smiles.*

"That's not my reindeer." She clapped her hands like a kid on Christmas morning in one of those sappy made-for-TV movies Alec always tried to avoid. "I can't believe it. That's not my reindeer! Problem solved."

Was she delusional? "What makes you think he's not yours?"

"Look." She waved a hand at Palmer. And it was most definitely Palmer. Alec would have recognized that obstinate animal anywhere. He had a white ring around one of his eyes, unlike any of the other reindeer in the herd.

"I'm looking..." He crossed his arms. "...at Palmer. Who belongs to you, I might add."

"It can't be Palmer. Isn't Palmer a boy reindeer?"

Alec had a feeling he knew where this was going. She'd expected a male reindeer to have a big rack of antlers. Most people did. Then again, most people were wrong, as was his new boss.

He bit back a smile. "Yes, Palmer is a male."

"Well, clearly this is a girl reindeer. See? No antlers." She did the clapping thing again. "Not my reindeer. Not my problem."

He laughed. "I hate to break it to you, but male reindeer shed their antlers after rutting season. During this time of year, female reindeer are the only ones with antlers, Miss Smarty Pants."

"Miss Smarty Pants?" She narrowed her gaze. The grit Alec saw there almost made him feel sorry for Palmer. "You think this is funny?"

"A little." His shoulders shook, but he had the good sense not to laugh out loud again.

"This is not a joke. I should...should..." She appeared to struggle for words. For once. "Oh, I don't know...fire you or something."

"*Fire* me?" Now he did laugh. Loud. And hard. "Go right ahead, sweetheart. I'm sure the fact that you can't tell the boy reindeer from the girls won't be a problem at all. Especially during rut."

She gave her hair a defiant toss over her shoulder. Alec was certain it was purely for dramatic effect since the arctic wind was swirling around them with increasing force. Palmer was already half buried in snow. "I could figure it out."

"I'm sure you could," he said with an ironic grin. "Things seem to be going so well for you on your first day of reindeer-farm ownership. I have no doubt it will all be smooth sailing from here. Why would you need me?"

She said nothing.

Alec should have stopped talking then and there. He wasn't sure why he didn't, except that Zoey had a way of making him forget to think. "In case you haven't noticed, no one else is out here helping you. Like it or not, I'm all you've got."

The moment the words left his mouth, he knew he'd crossed some sort of invisible boundary line.

She blinked at him, wide-eyed. Then Alec watched in horror as her chin wobbled, as if she might cry. That smallest of movements was enough to make him feel as if he'd just told some kid that Santa wasn't real.

He wished he could take the words back.

No. That was a lie. What he really wanted was to touch her. He had no idea where it came from, but he was overcome with the sudden desire to reach out and brush her cheek with the back of his hand.

What was happening to him? The altitude must be getting to him. Or the cold. He'd heard about people who'd suffered from hallucinations on the verge of freezing to death.

He'd been colder in his life. And he obviously wasn't close to freezing to death. So where were these thoughts coming from? Zoey was watching him now, which unnerved him even more. At least her chin had quit wobbling.

Thank You, God.

He frowned. He hadn't thought about God in a long time. Not since his Sunday-school days, which had been years ago. Maybe he really was losing it.

He shoved his hands in the pockets of his parka and strode past Zoey, toward Palmer.

"Come on. Let's do this," he muttered.

When he heard Zoey fall into step behind him in the snow, he wasn't altogether sure whether to feel troubled or relieved.

* * *

Like it or not, I'm all you've got.

Zoey didn't know why Alec's words affected her quite the way they did. It wasn't as though she didn't have anyone to lean on. There were plenty of people in Aurora who cared about her. And she could always count on the church. She knew that for a fact. Aurora Community Church had been there when she needed support most. Zoey herself now headed up their outreach program, so she knew firsthand the importance of the church's mission to reach out to the community.

But her various friends and the church weren't exactly at the forefront of her mind as she stared down the reindeer that seemed perfectly content to nap in the middle of the airport runway. A reindeer that apparently *did* belong to her, after all.

What was she doing? She'd thought she could power through this situation and solve the problem on her own. She'd even insisted that Clementine and Anya stay and finish their pedicures. She was accustomed to taking care of herself. She'd been doing it nearly half her life.

Clearly this time she was in over her head. But having Alec Wynn laugh at her was more than she could take. She'd reached the tipping point.

I should *fire him,* she thought as she tramped through the snow behind him. *I really should.* Was being mean grounds for termination? If not, it should be.

But the closer they got to Palmer, the less Zoey fantasized about ridding herself of Alec. The reindeer looked a lot bigger now that they were bearing down on him. Huge. And wooly. Zoey had seen reindeer up close and personal at Aurora's Reindeer Run every spring. But those reindeer looked smaller and sleeker, somehow. Maybe they were girls. Or just wimpy reindeer. Who knew?

Had she really thought she could get this massive, hairy

thing to budge all on her own? Maybe she would fire Alec *after* they moved Palmer out of the way.

"Scared?" Alec asked, as they stood a mere five feet away from the animal.

A little. "No," she said, doing her best to avoid his penetrating blue gaze.

He lifted a dubious brow. "There's nothing to be afraid of. Reindeer are more afraid of you than you are of them. If this was any other member of your herd, you could have come out here, waved your arms and yelled *shoo* and the problem would have been solved."

She wondered if it was the truth or if he was just trying to be nice. Then she remembered who was doing the talking. "So my strategy wasn't too far off the mark, then?"

"No, it wasn't." The corner of his mouth lifted into a half grin.

Zoey half relaxed. "Why won't that technique work on Palmer?"

"Because he's stubborn as a mule." His grin deepened, revealing a hint of a dimple on the right side of his face. "Just like someone else I've recently met."

"I'm not stubborn. I'm self-sufficient."

He pinned her with a sardonic look. "Keep telling yourself that, sweetheart."

Zoey's face grew warm, despite the flurry of snowflakes landing against her skin. She wished he'd quit calling her *sweetheart*...not that it sounded in any way complimentary. "So, what do we do now?"

"I have a secret weapon." He pulled a carrot from the pocket of his parka.

Zoey laughed. "Do you always run around with vegetables in your pockets?"

"On my one and only afternoon off?" He tossed the carrot in the air and caught it. "No, not usually. I stopped by the hotel kitchen just now. It was a necessary diversion."

"I wondered how you'd ended up out here." Guilt pricked her consciousness. He wasn't even on the clock. He'd probably been sitting inside drinking coffee or something when he'd heard about Palmer.

And here he was, with a pocketful of carrots.

Like it or not, I'm all you've got.

Something told her Alec Wynn might not be quite as dangerous as he looked.

"Hey there, bud," he called to Palmer. "What are you doing all the way out here?"

It was probably the sweetest tone she'd ever heard come out of his mouth. His voice could melt an ice floe.

Dangerous. Without a doubt.

Palmer rose to his feet—*hooves?*—with a grunt. He gave a shake like a dog after a bath, and snow flew anywhere and everywhere. He took a step closer to Alec and craned his neck toward the carrot.

Alec snapped the carrot in two and presented half of it to Palmer with an open palm. The reindeer appeared to inhale it.

While Palmer was crunching away, Alec offered the other half to Zoey. "Do you want to give it a try?"

"Yes! Please."

"Hold it in the palm of your hand and show it to him. Remember to keep your palm flat and your fingers together." He winked, and for some reason that word—*sweetheart*—floated around in Zoey's head. "Carrots look a lot like fingers."

She gulped as she stripped off one of her gloves. "Oh."

She might as well get used to it. Her reindeer weren't going anywhere, unless running wild through town counted. She was stuck with them.

You could still sell them, you know.

She pushed the thought away. While she was hand-feeding

him, it seemed cruel to even contemplate the notion of Palmer turning up on a menu somewhere.

The carrot rested on her open but somewhat shaky palm. Alec wrapped his fingers around her wrist and guided her hand to Palmer's head. The reindeer pressed his muzzle against her palm. It felt like velvet against her bare skin.

She laughed. "It tickles."

"Yeah, I guess it does." Alec met her gaze for a split second then looked away and released her wrist.

Zoey cleared her throat and shoved her hand back in her glove. "Now what?"

"Now we take the escape artist for a walk." He produced another carrot from his pocket and showed it to Palmer. "Come on, bud. There's more where the other one came from, but you've got to get out of the way first."

And just like that, Alec led Palmer off the runway and out of harm's way.

He made it look so simple.

A cheer rose from the crowd of pilots, airport personnel and other onlookers who'd gathered around the frozen lake to witness the spectacle. Zoey had been so caught up in the drama, she hadn't even noticed that half of Aurora had turned out to watch.

"Tell me that's not a news crew," she muttered under her breath.

"It's not a news crew." Alec chuckled. "Except that it is."

She was mortified. How was she supposed to gain any credibility as a brand-new charter pilot when one of her reindeer had shut down the entire airport?

You won't be a charter pilot if you can't make the down payment on that plane...

Five days. More like four, now that the sun was setting. A full moon had already risen high in the pink Alaskan sky. The horizon was bathed in a soft lavender glow that made the mountains resemble icing on a cake. How lovely it would have looked from the cockpit of a plane.

Zoey's eyes grew misty. What was she going to do? Palmer was under control for the time being, but it was a hollow victory. She still owed Alec a thousand dollars, and she still had thirty other reindeer to worry about. How was she ever going to afford all that, plus her airplane?

"You okay?"

Zoey glanced up at Alec, still leading Palmer around with a very literal dangling carrot. "A little overwhelmed, that's all. It's been a long day."

"Keep your chin up. Everyone will forget about this in a day or two." He kept his gaze glued to Palmer.

Zoey wasn't sure if he was worried about the reindeer bolting, or if he felt as uncomfortable delivering a pep talk as she did to be on the receiving end of it. "Just so we're clear, you're officially un-fired."

He let out a laugh. "You never fired me."

Hadn't she? She'd certainly meant to. "Yes, I did."

"No, you didn't." He glowered at her. "I can take this from here. Don't you have a pedicure to get back to or something?"

How on earth did he know about the pedicure? "I appreciate the concern, but my toes are fine."

He gave her another look filled with blue-eyed ire. "Are you walking back with us, or will you be arriving via your private plane?"

Just how had he spent his afternoon off? Investigating her? "It's not like you think. I'm not a spoiled heiress."

He shrugged. "So you keep saying." Zoey braced herself for another sarcastic *sweetheart*. It never came. She was almost disappointed.

She counted to ten before she did something stupid, like blurting out that he was fired again. Because clearly she needed him, as much as it pained her to admit it. By the time she got to five, they were engulfed in a throng of people. Zoey found herself with two television cameras and half a dozen microphones in her face. Everyone wanted a sound bite, something clever and quirky for the evening news. Because this was Alaska, where things like renegade reindeer made the front page—just one of the myriad reasons why she loved Aurora. She blinked against an assault of flashbulbs.

When her vision cleared, Alec and Palmer were nowhere to be seen.

Chapter Four

Zoey would be lying if she said she'd never fantasized about one day seeing herself on television. As nonsensical as it sounded, those fantasies usually involved winning an Oscar or a Grammy, and she was wearing an evening gown with sequins and maybe even a train. Never in her wildest dreams did she think the lead story on the local news would feature her escorting a reindeer off an airport runway. It seemed almost as ridiculous a notion as winning Best Supporting Actress or Best Female Vocalist.

Yet, there she was. In living color.

"You look lovely, dear." Kirimi, Anya's mother, waved the needle and thread in her hand toward the tiny television on the worktable at the church thrift store.

After the fiasco at the airport, Zoey had sought refuge here. She'd hoped going through boxes of newly donated clothes would take her mind off Palmer, the FAA and her rapidly accumulating debt.

And Alec Wynn.

"You sure do. Look how rosy your cheeks are." Anya nodded. Even standing side by side, it was difficult to see the resemblance between mother and daughter.

"You're glowing, Zoey. Glowing." Kirimi slid her needle

into a threadbare mitten. The things she could do with a needle and thread were nothing short of amazing.

Zoey's skills, on the other hand, were limited to organizing inventory and helping customers. She sometimes wondered if her mother would have taught her to sew, had she lived long enough. Then again, Anya wasn't exactly a whiz with a sewing machine. Up until the past year or so, she and her mom had had a strained relationship. That was difficult to believe seeing them now, volunteering side by side.

"As much as I appreciate your kind words, you two are nuts." Zoey couldn't even look at her onscreen self. "The entire experience was mortifying."

Except...

There'd been a moment out there on the ice—when Alec had delivered his uncomfortable pep talk—that had been sort of sweet.

Zoey swallowed. *He said one nice thing. And he couldn't even look at you when he said it. Get a grip on yourself.*

"We're just trying to put a positive spin on things." Anya shrugged. "Besides, you really do look good on TV."

Zoey forced herself to look at the television. There she was—standing beside Alec, who was dangling a carrot in front of Palmer. The reindeer looked so picturesque, his back lightly dusted with snow. Like something out of a Christmas movie.

Alec didn't look so bad himself.

Zoey absently folded something. A shirt? A sweater? Who knew? Alec looked absurdly handsome on-screen. Even more so than he did in person. No wonder the televised version of herself was gazing up at him as if he was the best thing to happen to Alaska since the Gold Rush. It was humiliating.

"I'm not glowing," she protested. "That's windburn."

"Sure it is," Kirimi said with an uncharacteristically saucy grin. "My Anya was right. Your reindeer man is rather dashing."

Reindeer Man. It sounded like a superhero.

Zoey rolled her eyes. Why was she always comparing Alec to superheroes? "He's not exactly mine."

"He works for you, so he sort of is." Anya winked.

Zoey knew Anya was only teasing, but the thought of anyone owning Alec Wynn was laughable. She wasn't sure why, but he struck her as the type of man who valued his freedom. Maybe it was the motorcycle.

"Shh." Anya grabbed the remote and turned up the volume on the TV. "They just said your name."

"The reindeer has been identified as the property of Zoey Hathaway, longtime Aurora resident. Subsequent to the animal's capture and removal from the airport, chief air-traffic-control officer Chuck Baker announced Ms. Hathaway will be assessed a fine for impeding air traffic and shutting down the airport. The amount of the fine, as determined by the Federal Aviation Administration, is two thousand dollars."

"What?" Zoey dropped the garment in her hands. A shirt, as it turned out.

"They're making you pay a fine? That's hardly fair. It wasn't your fault," Anya said. "I object."

Zoey objected, too. She objected to the fine. She objected to the fact that she had to learn about it on the evening news. She even objected to the wording of the news report.

Subsequent to the animal's capture? Wasn't that overly dramatic? There'd been no capture. He'd followed Alec and his carrot all the way back to the ranch. The reporter made it sound as though they'd shot him with a tranquilizer dart or something.

She refolded the shirt and grabbed another item from the cardboard box in the center of the table. Why was she worrying about semantics? She had more pressing problems to worry about right now. Two thousand of them. Three, counting the money she owed Alec.

"Try not to worry, dear." Kirimi gave her arm a gentle pat. The gesture was so unexpectedly maternal that it made Zoey's chest ache. "Maybe you can talk to Chuck and he'll reconsider."

"It's not Chuck's call. The fine is levied by the FAA. There's nothing more he can do. When I left the airport earlier, he told me he'd talk to them and recommend leniency. I know he did the best he could." If two thousand dollars was lenient, Zoey didn't even want to know what was standard.

"That's a lot of money." Anya grabbed the remote and turned off the television. The coverage had moved to the weather forecast.

Zoey didn't need a weatherman to tell her what she already knew—there would be snow. Inches and inches of snow. Par for the course for Alaska. Besides, she suddenly didn't feel like watching TV anymore.

"Is there anything we can do to help? What are you going to do, dear?" Kirimi asked.

Zoey stared, dazed, at the flannel shirt in her hands. It looked like something Gus would have worn, a thought that made her feel even worse. What could she do? Sell the reindeer? She didn't think she could. Not after today. But she couldn't give up her airplane, either.

Surely there was a way to work everything out. Christmas was coming. Her world couldn't fall to pieces right before Christmas. It just couldn't. "I'm going to do the only thing I can do. I'm going to pray. Harder than I've ever prayed before."

Alec stomped the snow from his work boots on the welcome mat and glanced at the modest sign above the shop door. *Aurora Community Church Thrift Store.* He wasn't so sure about the *church* part of the equation. He hadn't set foot in a church in years. Not since Camille had broken off their engagement.

But this was a store, not a church. And he needed a good pair of work gloves. This seemed as good a place as any, so he pushed the door open and stepped inside.

The instant he set foot in the crowded little store, an all-too-familiar, all-too-chipper voice rang out. "Welcome! How can I help you?"

Zoey.

She was everywhere all of a sudden. Just how small was this town? "Hi there, boss."

"Alec. Oh." In the split second before she composed herself, she didn't look any happier to see him than he was to see her. Before he could blink, she pasted a smile on her face. Ever the cheery princess.

Alec couldn't imagine how exhausting it must be to project such a bouncy, happy image to the world at all times. Just thinking about it made his head hurt. "You work here?"

"Sort of." She cast a glance over her shoulder, where a couple of other women stood behind a worktable, pretending not to listen if their not-so-subtle grins were any indication. One of them looked familiar.

Alec waved at them. "Ladies."

They waved back, and he realized that the younger of the two was the woman who'd accompanied Zoey to the ranch earlier.

He turned his attention back to Zoey. "So you 'sort of' work here? What exactly does that mean?"

"I'm a volunteer."

He rolled his eyes. "Of course you are."

"What's wrong with volunteering?" Her eyes flashed—a

telltale crack in her perfect, bubbly composure. She looked even prettier when she was flustered, he noted.

Then he reminded himself he shouldn't be noticing such things. "I never said there was anything wrong with it. It just seems like the type of thing you'd do, that's all."

She crossed her willowy arms, clearly an effort to physically hold her anger at bay. Alec couldn't help but wonder what she'd be like if she let it all out. "Why are you so insistent on pigeonholing me? I told you I'm not what you think."

His gaze swept her up and down, from her bouncy princess hair to the pompoms dangling from the ties of her snow boots. "Clearly not."

Color rose to her cheeks. She looked like the Tooth Fairy on the verge of a murderous rampage. "Why are you so mean? I should fire you. *Again.* You can't be the only man around here who knows about reindeer."

"I'll be happy to move on as soon as you say the word… and pay me the money you owe me, of course." Alec lifted an expectant brow.

He should cut her some slack. She'd obviously had a rough day. But there was something fun about rattling her. And Alec hadn't had much fun in his life.

"Is there an actual reason you stopped by, or was it purely to antagonize me?" she asked, refusing to take his bait.

He was beginning to suspect she didn't have the money. And if she didn't, then he'd indeed misjudged her.

I'm not your average heiress.

For some crazy reason, those words made him smile. "I need some work gloves."

"Right this way." She spun on her heel, moving through the crowded shelves of the thrift store with the energy of an arctic hare.

Alec followed, studiously averting his gaze from the sway

of her slender hips. No good could come from forming an appreciation for her figure.

His eyes flitted to her tiny waist.

Too late.

"Here we go." She stopped at a shelf located near the back of the shop. "Men's work gloves. We have three pairs to choose from. Take your pick."

He chose the tan-colored ones in the middle, the least worn-looking pair, and slid them on. "These look good. How much?"

"Um. Two dollars, I think." Zoey frowned all of a sudden. And if Alec wasn't mistaken, there was a slight tremor in her perfectly pink bottom lip.

He'd made her cry. Great. "Look, I'm sorry about before. I was just giving you a hard time. I think it's nice that you volunteer here. Very sweet. Really."

She blinked up at him with those sea-green eyes of hers, and Alec felt like the biggest jerk this side of the Lower 48.

"It's not that. It's the gloves...." She gestured toward the work gloves.

Who grew emotional over a pair of gloves?

He stared down at them. "Do they look that awful on me?"

She laughed, and the sound hit Alec's chest with a zing that was equal parts pleasure and pain. "No. It's just that they belonged to Gus."

The memory of finding Gus's lifeless body half-covered in snow hit Alec hard and fast. He closed his eyes, as if that could erase the image from his mind. As if anything could.

He breathed in and out, in and out, and opened his eyes. "Sorry. I didn't realize."

He began to pull them off, but before he could, Zoey's hands closed over his. "No. You keep them. You should have them. After all, you tried to save him."

His gaze moved from the odd sight of their interlocked

hands to her face, where he found her looking at him as if he were some kind of superhero. No one had ever looked at him quite like that before.

He wanted to tell her to stop. He actually preferred it when she looked at him with disdain. He hadn't done anything special or admirable. Ever. From day one, his life had been a mess. He wasn't her superhero. Hers or anyone's.

But the words wouldn't come. It was a struggle to simply say "thank you," press a couple of dollar bills into her hand and walk away.

Snow brushed against Alec's kneecaps as he walked the perimeter of the ranch the next morning, checking, double-checking and triple-checking the fence. Nearly a foot of fresh powder had fallen the night before, covering the farm in a blanket of dazzling white. Alec couldn't deny it was rather pretty, even when his toes grew numb and he lost sight of his feet.

Palmer had decided to give them all a break and spend the night at home where he belonged. He'd been one of the first deer to show up for breakfast, all bright-eyed and bushy-tailed, seemingly oblivious to the trouble he'd caused the day before. But Alec knew better than to trust the naughty reindeer. He could practically see the wheels turning behind Palmer's dark, almond-shaped eyes. He was formulating another escape plan. Alec was sure of it.

He shook his head as he poked his fingers through a square of the welded wire fence near the back corner of the pasture and checked for breakage. No doubt he was giving Palmer too much credit. Animals weren't like people. They didn't plot and plan, waiting for the perfect moment to run. More than likely, Palmer was an opportunist. When he saw a chance, he took it—just as Alec had done.

It had been a week before his high-school graduation.

He'd had an after-school job cleaning out cages at the local animal shelter. Grunt work. The kind of thing no one else wanted to do.

Alec didn't mind much. It was better than being at home, even though things had settled down somewhat. His father hadn't hit him in almost a year. Two months had passed since either his mother or father had used. Sixty-one days.

And Alec had started collecting paychecks. He'd thought he might even work full time once school was out and try to save enough money to get a place on his own. He'd already managed to squirrel away a few hundred dollars he kept hidden under his mattress in an old, beat-up Band-Aid box.

But that day he'd come home and found both his parents passed out on the living-room floor and the Band-Aid box empty. He would never forget the bottomless feeling that had come over him as he'd looked inside that rusty box, and the hot sting of tears on his cheeks when he realized just what all his hard-earned money had paid for. He'd cried like a little kid.

And then he'd just left. Right then. And he hadn't shed a tear since. Not even when Camille had called off their engagement.

It had been only days before Christmas when Camille slid his engagement ring off her finger. He'd foolishly thought his past was behind him, once and for all. He'd been honest. He'd told her about his parents as soon as they'd started dating. She'd been a Christian. Jesus was all about grace, right?

Somewhere around Thanksgiving, Camille had begun to have doubts. By the time stockings all over the world had been hung by the chimney with care, her family had gotten to her and convinced her those doubts were as real as the evergreen tree Alec had chosen at the Christmas-tree farm and tied to the roof of his car.

He'd forgotten all about the tree as he'd listened calmly to her explanation and accepted the ring she'd already removed and returned to him in a plain brown envelope. Then he'd walked right out the door. When he'd stepped outside and saw the evergreen strapped to the roof of his car, he nearly lost it. But he still hadn't cried. He'd driven straight to the dealership and traded his car in for a motorcycle that very day, tree and all.

He'd used up all his tears back when he was a teenager, the day he'd peered into that empty Band-Aid box and discovered his stash was gone. Without the missing money, he'd had only a few crumpled bills in his pockets. But it was enough to get him on a bus out of town. That bus had taken him to Port Angeles, on the edge of the Olympic Forest.

His first job in the forest had consisted of walking miles every day through the woodlands, marking trees for culling. The isolation of it suited him. Every morning he'd welcomed the opportunity to get lost in the woods. In the shade of the tree canopy, he'd felt far away from everything he'd left behind. He'd felt free. As free as he could feel, anyway.

Morning was still his favorite time of day. Especially quiet mornings like this one. He could hear nothing but the crunch of snow under his feet and the click of reindeer hooves behind him.

Palmer, of course.

Alec glanced over his shoulder. Just as he'd suspected, a certain reindeer with a white ring around his left eye was trailing his heels. "You know you can't sneak up on me. I can hear you clicking. You sound like an old man with creaky ankles."

Palmer's frosty white eyelashes fluttered. He was far from old. Alec's best guess was five or six years of age, which meant he had a good four years left. Maybe more. The clicking sound—caused by a tendon in their rear hooves—was universal among adult reindeer. It was nature's way of helping reindeer keep track of one another in blizzards. Or, in Alec's case, of knowing when one was shadowing him.

"If you're hoping I'm going to lead you to an opening in the fence, then you're sorely out of luck. You're going to have to find your own escape route."

Palmer's only response was a quiet grunt. And more eyelash fluttering.

Alec reached out and rested his palm on Palmer's muzzle. After only a day or two on the farm, Alec had learned how and when to pet the reindeer. They seemed to prefer being touched on the head or neck, with the nose being a particularly favorite spot. Some liked being petted more than others, but none of them craved attention like Palmer. Most of the time, he followed Alec around like a devoted puppy, which made his unpredictable disappearing acts all the more mystifying.

"What are you running from, bud?" Alec rubbed the pad of his thumb against Palmer's nose. It was covered in soft fuzz, a defense mechanism against frostbite. Palmer leaned into Alec's touch, looking as happy as could be.

Alec was stumped. He was certainly no expert in reindeer husbandry, but the animal seemed content. Why did he keep disappearing? And how was he managing it? The fence was 100 percent intact. Alec had looked at every square inch of it.

"You don't have it so bad around here, you know," he muttered. "Trust me on this."

He dropped his hand back to his side and searched Palmer's expression one last time.

It was no use. He was no reindeer mind reader.

He trudged through the snow back toward the barn. Palmer's tendency to roam hadn't been a problem up until now. He'd managed to keep out of trouble on his previous excursions, but taking a nap at the airport was obviously out of the question. And even though it technically wasn't his problem, Alec felt responsible.

Behind him, Palmer's hooves clicked, an audible reminder of his predicament.

Not my *predicament. Zoey's.*

He scowled. Why he wanted to help her was beyond him. He didn't owe her anything. In fact, quite the opposite. One thousand times the opposite, give or take a nickel. And it wasn't as though she welcomed his assistance. She'd made it more than clear that she could take care of things on her own.

Yeah, right.

She took the whole rose-colored glasses thing to a new level. But much to his chagrin, he found her unwavering spunkiness nearly as appealing as it was annoying. Given his past, he could appreciate a feisty, independent streak. Even if that independent streak was a little nutty.

And she was kinda cute.

There, he'd admitted it. It wasn't as if he would do anything about it. *It* being her cuteness. He'd been down that road before. He had no inclination to go down it again. And he was more than certain that he wasn't Zoey's type. If she knew what was good for her, she'd avoid him like the plague.

He inhaled a lungful of arctic air as the log-cabin-style barn came into view. He felt better somehow. The quiet, peaceful morning stretched out before him, and his head felt clearer. Wasn't admitting the existence of a problem always the first step? He'd admitted his quasi-attraction to Zoey Hathaway. Now he could forget all about her and move on.

He pushed through the back door, and in an instant his visions of a calm, stress-free morning evaporated. Through the wide double doors on the opposite side of the barn, Zoey strode toward him. Her blond hair was swept up in a high, perky ponytail, and her arms were piled high with three cardboard boxes.

Yep...cute.

Alec grimaced and stuffed his hands in his pockets to

stop himself from snagging a box or two off the top of her pile. "Hello."

She jumped. "Oh. Alec. You frightened me."

Good. I should frighten you. "Sorry."

"What are you doing here?" She loosened her arms and let the boxes slide to the ground.

She just let them sit there…all that cardboard in the wet snow. Like Palmer, those boxes weren't Alec's problem. But they worked his last nerve all the same.

He scooped them up. "This is my place of employment, remember? Or am I fired again?"

"No. Not yet, anyway." She flushed. She tended to do that a lot, he'd noticed. "Do you always get here so early in the morning?"

"I live on the property. Room and board is included with my salary." He jerked his head in the direction of the small guest cabin adjacent to the barn.

It was pretty bare—a twin bed, a bathroom and a glorified hot plate for a kitchen. But Alec didn't mind. He'd lived in far worse conditions. When he'd first moved to the Olympic Forest, he'd lived outdoors in a tent. That was years ago, but the experience had given him an appreciation for life's little luxuries. Things like central heating, indoor plumbing and a soft place to rest.

No doubt Zoey wouldn't understand such worries. Not many people did.

"I see." Her gaze strayed toward the guest cabin, his motorcycle parked out front and then back to him.

He nodded at the pyramid of boxes in his arms. "Where should I take these, boss?"

Upon his use of the word *boss,* her flush intensified. "Into the house, of course."

"The house?"

"Yes." She nodded, and her ponytail bobbed gleefully up and down. "Today's moving day."

So much for his peaceful, solitary mornings.

Alec wasn't sure why he'd never entertained the possibility that Zoey would move into Gus Henderson's home. It *was* hers now. But he'd never once imagined her actually living there, particularly so soon. "You don't waste any time, do you?"

"I was actually planning on moving anyway. While I was working at the coffee bar, the Northern Lights Inn gave me a room as part of my pay. This past Friday was my last day."

He lifted an irritated brow. "So you don't have a job?"

The way Alec saw it, her unemployed status meant one of two things—either she was rich or he'd never see the money she owed him. She'd already denied being wealthy on multiple occasions, so he assumed it was the latter.

Goodbye, one thousand dollars. He may as well have fed twenties and fifties straight to the reindeer.

"Not exactly." She bit her bottom lip.

Alec's attention would have probably snagged on that lip had he not been so busy thinking about how aggravated he was with her. "It's a simple question—do you have a job? Yes or no?"

"No." She squared her slender shoulders. "Not at the moment."

Why didn't this information come as a surprise? Alec shifted the boxes in his arms and marched toward the house.

"I know what you're thinking," Zoey said, trailing behind him.

"I doubt that," he ground out.

"You're worried about the money I owe you."

Not so much worried as mourning the loss of it. "Convince me I shouldn't be concerned. Please."

They'd reached the side porch of the little log cabin where

Gus Henderson had once lived. Zoey dug a key out of the pocket of her parka and slipped it in the lock on the door. Once inside, Alec dropped the boxes on the round, rustic pine kitchen table.

Then he crossed his arms and waited.

"Look, I have your money. All of it. I can write you a check right now if you like." Zoey prayed that wasn't what he expected. At least not until she'd had a chance to convince him otherwise. "But I have a proposal for you."

"A proposal?" His eyes narrowed.

A *proposal.*

Zoey's stomach fluttered. Couldn't she have chosen another word? One less matrimonial? "I'm talking about a payment arrangement."

He sank into one of the kitchen chairs, stretched his long legs out in front of him and crossed his feet at the ankles. "I'll take my check now, thanks."

The conversation wasn't going quite as Zoey had planned. After a night of tossing, turning and more prayers than she'd uttered in as long as she could remember, she'd gotten up early and rehearsed exactly what she would say to Alec. And now she'd forgotten every word. It was too hard to concentrate with him here, filling up the room with his overwhelming intensity.

She closed her eyes. Perhaps she could manage to string a few coherent words together when she wasn't looking at him. "I don't want the reindeer to end up as hot dogs."

"Zoey?" His voice sounded different from how it had before. Softer. Softer, but still very Alec. "Open your eyes."

Her lashes fluttered open.

He stood and pulled out a chair. "Sit."

She obeyed.

"Why don't you tell me what's going on?" There it was again—that barely perceptible hint of softness in his tone.

It was all the invitation she needed. She told him all about the offer for the reindeer, the fine from the FAA and, finally, about her plane. "It's not anything fancy, just a prop plane. But it would be *my* prop plane. I've dreamed of becoming a charter pilot since I was sixteen years old."

She stopped. She couldn't tell him about her parents. Not yet. She told herself it was because they'd only known each other for two rather turbulent days. But deep down, she wondered if the real reason she couldn't was because she feared what would happen once she did. He might look at her like everyone else did, as if she was a charity case or a tragic little sister who needed taking care of. She didn't want Alec Wynn's sympathy. And she most definitely didn't want to be his kid sister.

She gulped. Of course she wasn't his sister. She was his boss. And nothing more.

"You're a pilot?" The corner of his mouth lifted, and his face bore the oddest expression—a curious mixture of bewilderment and amusement.

"Does that surprise you?"

He gave her a rare smile. "No, frankly. It doesn't surprise me a bit."

Zoey liked that answer. She liked it a lot. So much so that it scared her a little.

She cleared her throat. "Getting back to business..."

"Business." The set of his jaw hardened, and the look in his eyes grew distant. "Of course."

Whatever fleeting moment of tenderness they'd shared had passed, exactly as she'd planned. Zoey should have been pleased. Instead, she felt inexplicably hollow. "Can I have a little more time to reimburse your out-of-pocket expenses?"

He waited an excruciating beat before asking, "How long?"

She smiled—a weak attempt at softening the blow. "I was thinking until Christmas."

It seemed like a reasonable deadline. Gus had paid Alec's salary through the end of the year. After then, it would be Zoey's responsibility. She needed to eradicate her debt to him before she owed him even more money.

He glanced out a big bay window overlooking the pasture. The reindeer were clustered together in a large group, lying down in the snow. Zoey couldn't help but notice that some of the tension left Alec's features as he watched them. "I suppose I could make that work, seeing as I'm the only thing standing between the herd and a side of relish."

He wasn't the only thing…there was still the FAA fine to worry about. But getting Alec to agree to this arrangement was a start. Maybe now she wouldn't feel so nervous around him all the time. "We have a deal, then? Christmas?"

He nodded. "Christmas."

She beamed at him in return.

For the first time in forty-eight hours, Zoey could breathe without her chest aching. Christmas was three weeks away. Surely she could turn things around by then.

She had to.

Chapter Five

The entire population of Aurora turned out to help Zoey move into Gus Henderson's house. Or so it seemed to Alec. By midday there were more people pitching in than there were actual possessions to be moved. It was mind-boggling.

And disruptive.

Alec couldn't turn around without being introduced to someone. By the third or fourth handshake, he realized that most of the helpers were part of some sort of church group. And apparently Zoey was their fearless leader. Or at least some sort of high-ranking official.

Like a princess, for instance.

It wasn't exactly a bombshell revelation. Zoey appeared to think she could do anything, much of it all on her own. Why would something as daunting as saving the world be any different?

Alec rolled his eyes as he heaved a small bale of hay on top of the stack in the corner of the barn. Let her save the world. So long as she wasn't trying to save him, they'd get along fine. She seemed to have enough on her plate, however, so he assumed he wasn't anywhere on her radar.

A vague sense of disappointment nagged at him as he tossed another bale of hay on the pile, which tipped his disappointment into irritation. Why should he care what Zoey thought of him, or *if* she thought of him at all? He didn't spend his time thinking about *her.*

Except for now, you idiot...

And a good percentage of your waking hours.

A voice cut through the dim light of the barn. "Can I give you a hand?"

Alec turned and found Brock Parker standing in a sliver of pale pink sunlight drifting through the back door of the barn. He wore the same parka that had been slung over his chair at the coffee bar, but this time Alec's attention was drawn to a big white cross that was stitched across Brock's chest. As Alec took in the cross, along with the words Search & Rescue spelled out beneath it, recognition dawned.

Brock Parker had been at Olympic Forest. Not long. Just a day or two. He'd headed up a team that looked for a missing boy who'd wandered off from his family's campsite. In the end, the boy had been located safe and sound, with only a mild case of hypothermia.

But the day remained seared in Alec's memory—not only because of the notable rescue, but also because it had overlapped with the arrival of his father. He'd come out of the forest late one evening and found his father waiting for him at the park-ranger headquarters. He'd wanted money, of course. Some things never changed.

During the long ride from Washington to Alaska, Alec had revisited that day time and again, wondering if he'd done the right thing. In his haste to just somehow get his dad out of the park and away from the curious stares of his coworkers, he'd pressed a few dollar bills into his father's shaky, sweaty hand. *Please leave,* he'd said through clenched teeth. *Just go.*

Fat chance.

Deep down, Alec knew he'd be back. Why not? His efforts had been successful. So Alec had been the one to go. Just like before.

Brock had been there that day. What were the odds? Brock hadn't known him then, so it was doubtful he'd noticed anything amiss. But the possibility lingered, making Alec even less comfortable than he'd already been. Was it too much to ask to find a place where no one knew who he was or where he'd come from? A place where he could be whomever he wanted to be? Apparently so.

His gaze dropped to the dog at Brock's feet—the same one that had been curled beneath his chair at the coffee bar. He wondered if it was the same dog that had found the missing boy in the forest. Possibly. It was copper-colored with a white chest, as the other one had been. When Alec met the dog's gaze, its tail beat happily against Brock's legs.

"Thanks, but things are pretty much under control." Alec cast a halfhearted glance at the hay. There really wasn't much to be done here. In fact, hay was in short supply. They'd need more by the week's end.

Another expense for Zoey.

He swallowed. *Not your problem.*

Brock lingered in the doorway but made no move to enter the barn. "Avoiding the crowd?"

"Something like that." Something *exactly* like that.

How many people did it take to move a few boxes? From what he'd seen, Zoey didn't have all that many things. He wondered if her friends knew how uncomfortable she felt to be on the receiving end of all that help. Doubtful. But Alec could see it in the way she flitted around like a nervous butterfly, checking on one person after the next.

A nervous, beautiful butterfly.

Even now that butterfly was tucked in the kitchen of the log cabin making sandwiches for the whole crew.

"I can respect the feeling. Aurora's a small town with a

big heart. It can be overwhelming for a newcomer. Trust me. I've been there." Brock gave him a knowing smile. "I'll leave you to it, then."

Alec should have let him go. He'd come to the barn searching for a little peace and quiet, and he wasn't sure exactly what Brock remembered of him, if he remembered him at all.

But Alec's attention had snagged on the dog.

He had an idea. It was probably crazy. But no less crazy than chasing a runaway reindeer all over town.

"Can I ask you something?" he said to Brock's retreating back.

Brock stepped back into the barn. The dog mirrored his every movement, its paws moving in perfect sync with Brock's feet. "Sure."

Alec motioned toward the dog with a jerk of his head. "Did you train him yourself?"

"Watson here?" Brock's face split into a grin as he looked down at the dog. "For the most part, yes. My wife is also very involved with our training program."

"What kind of training program?"

Brock shrugged. "Search and rescue mostly. We specialize in mountain rescues—avalanches and bringing injured skiers off the slopes."

Not exactly what Alec had in mind. He didn't want to give up on his idea quite yet, though. "Do you ever train dogs for other types of work?"

Brock took a step closer, as did Watson. "What exactly are we talking about?"

"Don't laugh." Alec studied Watson's appearance. He looked like a regular dog. But so had the dog that had found the little boy. If a dog could find a missing kid, couldn't one also keep a reindeer in line? "I was thinking of a sheepdog, only for reindeer."

Brock's grin spread, but he didn't laugh. Alec considered that a good sign. "A reindeer-herding dog?"

"Does such a thing exist?" It had to. Dogs herded other animals all the time, not just sheep. Alec had even seen a dog herd a bunch of ducks once on television.

Brock shook his head. "Honestly, I don't know. I could do some research, make some calls. I know a few people with herding dogs."

"We've got a reindeer that's a bit of a problem." Alec glanced over Brock's shoulder, toward the pasture. Palmer was clustered with the other reindeer—*for now*—his legs curled beneath him, blinking against the snow.

"Yeah, Palmer. I'm aware. The whole town is aware." Now Brock did laugh, not that Alec could blame him.

"I thought maybe a sheepdog…er, reindeer dog…might be able to keep him in line. Or at least keep him from wandering." Alec pulled off his gloves and tossed them on the dwindling stack of hay.

"It's an idea. A creative one. I'll give you that."

Creativity aside, it was the only idea he had, short of tethering Palmer with a halter and a lead rope. But he had a feeling that wouldn't last long, either. If a metal fence couldn't keep the reindeer in check, it didn't seem as if a rope would cut it. And Alec didn't like the tethering idea in theory, either. It seemed cruel. Freedom was a concept he held near and dear, even for reindeer.

Alec raked a hand through his hair. He'd worked up a sweat in the barn, even though it was still so cold he could see his breath in the air. "But do you think it could work?"

"I haven't a clue. But it'll sure be fun to give it a shot." Brock grinned.

Fun.

It was so foreign an idea, Alec had trouble digesting the word. Not that there was anything wrong with fun. But he'd been so busy building a new life for himself for so long, he couldn't remember the last time he'd had a good time.

Helping Zoey yesterday was pretty fun.

He frowned. That was neither here nor there.

He directed his attention to Brock again. "Um, one more thing..."

Brock shrugged a shoulder. "Name it."

He was so relaxed. Friendly. Alec was tempted to bring up the rescue at Olympic and tell him they'd met before.

He would...

Later.

At best, bringing up the past would only lead to questions. Questions such as why Alec had left Washington and why he'd come all the way to Alaska. And those were questions he didn't feel like answering.

At worst, Brock already knew the answers to those questions.

"Could we keep this between us?" Alec asked. "For now at least?"

"Sure." Brock's gaze darted briefly to the house, where Zoey was no doubt making enough sandwiches to feed an army. "Is this a Christmas surprise?"

Alec grew still. A Christmas surprise? For Zoey? Hardly.

This wasn't a gift, Christmas or otherwise. He was merely trying to help. Zoey obviously needed it. Did she really think she could come up with his money by Christmas? Even if she did, what would happen afterward? Was he supposed to work for free? If he had half a brain in his head, he'd start looking for another job instead of trying to find a dog to babysit a reindeer.

He crossed his arms across his chest. "I just don't want to get her hopes up. That's all."

"Whatever you say. I understand." Brock's bemused expression told Alec he clearly didn't. "It'll be our secret."

* * *

"We've boxed up Gus's clothes, and they're all ready to take back to the thrift store." Anya sidled up next to Zoey in the kitchen. "Your things are all unpacked and your bed is made."

Even though it made little sense, Zoey felt almost guilty for getting rid of Gus's clothes—as though she was pushing him out of his home. But the thrift store raised money for people out in the bush, who had trouble affording even basic medical care. Gus's clothes would be put to good use.

She looked up from spreading peanut butter on a quartet of bread slices lined up on the counter. "Please tell me you're the one who organized my dresser drawers. I don't think I could look the youth pastor in the eye if I knew he'd been folding my socks."

"I could tell you that, but I'd be lying." Anya reached for the jar of plum jam and twisted the lid open.

"Seriously?" Zoey groaned.

She was grateful for the help. She really was. But it wasn't as though she had so many things that she couldn't have handled the move on her own. Her apartment at the Northern Lights Inn had been furnished. She had a few knickknacks that had belonged to her parents that were obviously precious to her, along with her clothes, which were fairly bulky, this being Alaska. An easy move, as far as moves went.

"Relax. Clementine handled your socks. She and I took charge of your bedroom." Anya slid the jam across the counter toward her, along with a clean knife. "A freakishly large number of your socks are red, by the way."

Zoey cut her a look.

"Sorry." Anya shrugged. "I couldn't help but notice."

"I like red."

"Then you've landed in the right place—a reindeer farm.

It will be like Christmas year-round." Anya glanced out the window over the sink.

Zoey followed her gaze. Three of the reindeer were chasing one another through the pasture, zipping from one end of the fence to the other. All three sported large racks of antlers, which meant they were females, Zoey noted. She knew that much now, thanks to Alec.

Without even thinking about it, she scanned the horizon for a glimpse of her broad-shouldered, temperamental employee. And came up empty.

The way he kept disappearing on her was annoying. And the fact that it annoyed her only annoyed her further. She twisted the lid back on the jar of peanut butter with a bit too much force.

"Look at that. They're goading one another," Anya said.

Goading one another?

Oh, yes…the reindeer. Zoey redirected her thoughts away from Alec and back toward her thirty-one newest friends. The majority of them were now up and running in an enthusiastic game of chase. The few that hadn't joined in the game were busy tossing hay around with their antlers, dotting the pristine canvas of snow with flecks of green.

The whole scene was awfully charming, even if it was all too easy for Zoey to picture the green they flung about as dollar bills instead of hay. "I talked to Alec this morning about the money I owe him," she said absently, her financial worries never far away.

Anya's eyes grew wide. "And?"

"And he agreed to give me until Christmas to pay him back."

"That's great." Anya grinned, leaned against the kitchen counter and crossed her feet at the ankles. "So he's not quite as tough as he looks. I knew it."

"Knew what, exactly?" Eager for a distraction from the

topic of conversation, Zoey went back to work assembling the sandwiches.

"I knew he'd be reasonable."

That makes one of us. "Now I just have to convince the FAA to wait for their money, as well."

"I'm sure Chuck can put in a good word for you."

"I might have used up all my goodwill with Chuck. I've called him a few times already today and keep getting his voice mail." Zoey gnawed on her lip. If she could get rid of this houseful of people, she could head over to the airport and deal with the FAA fine.

Good grief, what was happening to her? She was blessed with an abundance of people who wanted to come to her aid. She would feed them and socialize, like a normal, decent person. The FAA and its hefty fine would still be there tomorrow.

Unfortunately.

"Forgive me, Lord," she murmured under her breath. Then for good measure, she added an extra dollop of peanut butter to one of the sandwiches.

"Everything is going to work out." Anya waved a hand in the direction of the living room, where five people were unpacking a single box of books and adding them to the shelves that lined the walls of the log cabin. "You have so many people who want to help you. Let them."

"What are you suggesting? That I go in there and pass around a collection plate?" The idea was beyond mortifying. And it would never happen. Never ever.

To Zoey's horror, Anya's eyes lit up with enthusiasm. "That's a really good idea."

She couldn't be serious.

The blood drained from Zoey's face, and she was forced to lean against the counter for support. "I would rather die. Anya Parker, don't you dare go in there and ask anyone for money on my behalf."

Anya held up her hands in surrender. "Just hear me out. I'm not suggesting a collection plate. Obviously, that's a little extreme. But maybe you could put donation stations around town. Mason jars or something. With cute little signs that say Save the Reindeer. That's what this is about, right? Saving the reindeer?"

Zoey gave a slow nod. "Save the reindeer. I like it."

Save the reindeer.

Save her airplane.

And save her sanity.

"Excellent! We can get to work on it right away."

"Get to work on what?" Brock wandered into the kitchen, and his gaze zeroed in on the sandwiches at once.

"Here," Zoey said, handing him one. "Your wife is concocting a plan. I'm beginning to think she might be an evil genius."

"I could have told you that a long time ago." He winked at Anya and took a bite of PB and J.

"Hey." Anya nudged Brock with her hip. "I'll accept the *genius* label. But *evil?* I think not."

He leaned toward Anya and gave her what had to be a peanut-buttery smack on the lips. "We're just teasing you, sweetheart."

Sweetheart.

It sounded a lot nicer coming from Brock's mouth than it did from Alec's. But the memory of it caused Zoey's cheeks to flare with warmth anyway.

Anya wrapped her arms around Brock in a bear hug. They were sweet together. They always had been. But sometimes, lately, being around them made Zoey's heart ache.

She looked elsewhere, focusing intently on the jar of peanut butter. She wondered idly if reindeer liked peanut butter. And if so, did they prefer crunchy or smooth?

Reindeer and peanut butter? I'm losing it for sure.

"Where have you been, Brock? I feel like I haven't seen you for hours," Anya said.

"I was out in the barn chatting with Alec."

"Oh?" Zoey asked, her head snapping to attention quicker than she could stop it.

Her cheeks blazed, and she prayed neither Brock nor Anya had noticed her sudden change in demeanor.

"You find that interesting, Zoey?" Brock asked.

Anya observed their exchange with keen curiosity.

"No. Not particularly," Zoey answered, struggling to keep her hands steady as she cut the sandwiches in half. "My concern is for the reindeer."

Aurora was a small town. The last thing she needed was for word to get around that she harbored a secret crush on her ranch hand. Because she didn't. She just wondered what Brock and Alec would have to talk about. That was all.

Alec was nothing like anyone Zoey had ever known. He was a far cry from the solicitous—if sometimes nosy—people of Aurora. He was cynical, aloof and blunt to a fault. And she knew nothing of his past—where he came from, how he'd ended up in Alaska. She'd been acting as though he were an actual superhero when, in fact, he could be just the opposite. So what if those blue eyes of his sent her head reeling? And so what if, every now and then, he was kind and generous when she least expected it?

She'd done just fine on her own all these years. And now she had a pasture full of new buddies to keep her company. She needed a man in her life like she needed to inherit another herd of wild animals. Least of all a man like Alec Wynn.

The idea was laughable....

So why wasn't she laughing?

Chapter Six

Zoey felt like an impostor as she looked around the inside of her new home.

Her friends had all gone home hours ago. A fire burned in the hearth, and its amber flames cast dancing shadows on the knotty-pine walls of the cozy living room. The house was a traditional log cabin, built by Gus himself years ago, according to what the lawyer had told her. The furniture was simple—a red checkered sofa, broad teak coffee table and worn braided rug. The walls were mostly bare, which showcased the warm, one-of-a-kind quality of the wood. And it was lovely in its rustic simplicity. Strong. Humble. Charming.

Just like Gus.

Zoey's throat grew thick. She didn't deserve this. She wasn't Gus's family. Wasn't there someone else out there who should be here instead?

She ran her fingertips along one of the bookshelves that flanked the fireplace. It was crammed full. She recognized a few aviation books that Gus had loaned her at one time or another, but there wasn't a single picture frame. No photos of family or friends. Just books.

This was all he had. The cabin, the reindeer. Even his plane hadn't really belonged to him. He'd leased it. He had nothing but the farm. And now it was hers.

She squeezed her eyes shut.

Please, Lord. Help me find a way to take care of all this. For Gus.

She inhaled a ragged breath. She didn't want to cry. She didn't want to grieve. Not again. Not ever again.

She needed to get busy. To do something. Maybe she could find some mason jars in the kitchen and get to work on the Save the Reindeer campaign. Or better yet, check on the reindeer. She wouldn't have any idea what exactly she was checking for, but it would keep her mind off Gus.

She slipped on her parka and paused on her way out the door, wondering if she would run into Alec outside. She hadn't seen him in hours, since before the church group had arrived to help with the move. Once again, she'd been thrust into the role of the helpless orphan.

She chastised herself. It really wasn't fair to look at it that way. But having everyone pitch in on her behalf made her feel like a victim. As she had in the early days after the deaths of her parents—lost. And she hated feeling that way.

She pushed such thoughts from her mind and strode to the kitchen with purposeful steps then grabbed a few of the left-over sandwiches and wrapped them in a paper towel. She'd never eat them all herself, so she might as well share them with Alec. If he was around.

She glanced out the small window over the sink. His motorcycle was parked at a jaunty angle behind the barn. The seat and handlebars were covered with snow, but here and there she caught a glimpse of chrome glinting in the moonlight.

He's here somewhere, she mused. *Good.* Not that she had any particular desire to see him; she just didn't like the thought of him riding around on that thing in the dark. It seemed unduly dangerous in snowy conditions. Something bad could happen.

No more grieving.

For some mysterious reason, her heart clenched.

She hardly knew Alec. Why was she worried about his safety?

Because without him, you really would be lost these days. It was an unpleasant yet undeniable truth.

Zoey tried not to think about how much she really did need him as she shrugged into her parka. She tucked her hands into a pair of mittens, grabbed the sandwiches and headed outside.

The temperature had dropped quite a bit since she'd bid goodbye to the last of her helpers. Icicles dripped from the edge of the rooftop and snow swallowed her footsteps as she made her way to the fence. A shiver ran through her. But she forgot the weather as soon as she caught sight of the herd in the distance.

The reindeer were gathered together near the base of the mountain, dots of dark purple against the lavender hue of the snowy nighttime landscape. Most were lying down with their legs tucked beneath them, but a few stood, leaning into the wind. Snow swirled around them, and a gray cloud of vapor hung suspended over their heads, hiding the tips of their antlers.

Goose bumps prickled the back of Zoey's neck. She shuddered, but not from the cold.

"They really are a sight to behold," she whispered.

"Trouble sleeping?" Alec's voice was a low rumble as he sauntered up beside her.

"Oh." She turned toward him, her heart thumping hard in her chest. "Hi. You scared me. Again."

He angled his head toward her. "You're not accustomed to having someone around."

It was a statement, not a question. And it was said with

the assurance of someone who knew her well, which Alec obviously didn't. Couldn't.

"I guess I'm not." She dropped her gaze to the snow collecting on the fence post. Alec had a way of looking at her that made her feel transparent, and standing beside him in the darkness only exacerbated the sensation.

"Sorry," he murmured.

"Don't be." She cleared her throat and forced herself to look him in the eyes. Why was she suddenly feeling so flustered? Hadn't she come out here looking for him? "I was actually hoping to run into you. I just got distracted."

He nodded toward the reindeer. "I can't blame you. They make a pretty picture at night, don't they?"

"Gorgeous." She glanced at the reindeer. More goose bumps. If she didn't know better, she would have thought she and Alec had stepped into a Christmas movie.

Visions of mistletoe danced in Zoey's head. Her throat grew thick.

"You okay?" Alec gave her a sideways glance.

"Sure. Why wouldn't I be?" She shrugged and feigned nonchalance.

Mistletoe? Where had that come from?

He narrowed his gaze. "You said you were looking for me. Any particular reason?"

"I never said I was looking for you." She shook her head with a little too much vigor. "I said I was hoping to run into you. There's a difference."

"Is there, now?" The corner of his mouth lifted. Was that a smirk?

Yes. Yes, it was. Zoey wanted to dive into the nearest snowdrift.

"Here." She shoved the sandwiches at him, her hand colliding with a wall of firm, masculine chest.

He took the paper-towel-wrapped package and eyed it with suspicion. "What's this?"

"Sandwiches." Her cheeks—numb from the cold only moments before—burned.

He turned the bundle over, examining it. "That's awfully nice. Thank you."

"You're welcome." Why did she feel so awkward all of a sudden? She hadn't felt this self-conscious when she was handing them out to half the town earlier. "I mean, it's nothing, really. They're left over from this afternoon. And I thought you might be hungry."

Not to mention the fact that she was indebted to him. Literally.

"Earlier. Right." His gaze met hers and once again she felt exposed…vulnerable, for some odd reason.

She turned back toward the reindeer. "So, where do they sleep?"

Alec shrugged. "Right here."

"They're not too cold?" She glanced behind her. "What about the barn? Shouldn't we tuck them in there, away from the elements?"

"The barn is for the summertime, to keep them out of the heat. They do best in the cold. Their bodies are built for it. They can even lower the temperature in their legs to just above freezing, so they don't lose body heat."

Zoey shook her head. "How do you know all this?"

"Easy. Google." His lips curved into another of his rare smiles. "Don't worry. You'll catch on. Before I came here, I didn't know much about them, either."

She started to ask him what he'd done with himself when he lived in Washington, but before she could, he changed the subject.

"How did the move go?"

"Fine. What happened to you? You disappeared once everyone showed up."

His gaze drifted to the barn. "I was busy."

"Busy hiding from social interaction?" She lifted a brow. Surely he didn't think she hadn't noticed that he bordered on antisocial.

"Jealous?" His blue eyes glittered in the moonlight. And there was that smirk again.

"Jealous?" Was he serious? "Of what?"

"Of my hiding place." His smirk intensified. She was beginning to regret giving him the sandwiches.

"Please." She rolled her eyes.

"You can pretend all you want, but I saw how uncomfortable you were when the welcoming committee descended." He leaned his elbows on the fence and looked out at the horizon. The reindeer were as still and quiet as if they were pretty pictures on a Christmas card.

Zoey bit her lip. "Was it that obvious?"

She'd feel awful if anyone else had noticed. As much as she loathed playing the role of town orphan, she hated the thought of hurting anyone's feelings even more.

"No." Alec's voice grew soft, as it had when he'd coaxed her into telling him about the commercial farm's offer to purchase the reindeer.

As mysterious as he'd been when she'd first laid eyes on him—angry, intense, clad head to toe in black, straddling that monster of a motorcycle—he was even more so now. Quiet. Contemplative. If Zoey hadn't known better, she might have thought that somewhere beneath Alec's gruff exterior beat a sensitive heart.

"I might be more adept than most at recognizing an independent spirit," he said.

"You mean, it takes one to know one?" She smiled. "That sort of thing?"

"I suppose you could say so." He glanced at her, and something in his penetrating blue eyes was so poignant that Zoey's breath caught in her throat. "You don't like accepting help from people. You'd rather handle things on your own. Why is that?"

He'd gone from completely misjudging her to honing in on her biggest insecurity. How did he do it? She was almost nostalgic for the days when he'd thought she was a spoiled princess.

She took a deep breath and let the words flow. "I lost my parents when I was sixteen."

It felt strange saying it aloud. She hadn't actually had to tell anyone about her past before. Everyone in Aurora knew her story.

She peered up at him through the fringe of her eyelashes, fully expecting to see sympathy etched in his chiseled features. Or worse, pity. Relief coursed through her when she didn't.

He simply looked at her as though she was the same Zoey and he was the same Alec. As if nothing had changed. So she continued. "I guess you could say the whole town came together to take care of me. And they've been taking care of me ever since. Don't misunderstand—I appreciate all the love and support. I just…"

She stopped, unsure how to continue. How could she possibly put it into words?

Silence hung heavy between them until Alec spoke. And when he did, somehow he gave voice to the feelings Zoey couldn't. "You don't want to be that person for the rest of your life. You want to start over."

"Exactly." She turned her bewildered gaze toward him. How could someone who was barely more than a stranger seem to know her so well? "How did you…?"

He cut her off with another wistful look. "Just a hunch."

A hunch? She doubted that.

"What happened to your parents, if you don't mind my asking?" He unwrapped the sandwiches, took a giant bite of the one on top and put the others in his pocket.

The ordinariness of the gesture was somehow comforting. She could almost believe they were talking about any trivial matter, rather than her life's defining moment. She wondered if he'd done it on purpose.

Surely not. This was Alec—the man who'd hidden from her church group all day in the barn. He wasn't exactly a people person.

"They were in a plane crash," she said, once again surprised at how easily the words slipped from her mouth. "A twin-engine prop plane. They got caught in a surprise mountain downdraft."

She probably could have left that part out, but it was important to her that he knew it wasn't her father's fault. It was just an accident. A tragic, heartbreaking accident.

"Plane crash?" His brow furrowed.

"Yep." She shoved her hands in the pockets of her parka and waited for him to pronounce her crazy.

"And now you're a pilot?"

"Go ahead. Say it. You think I'm nuts." A smile danced on her lips, which should have seemed odd given the topic of conversation. Somehow it didn't. Talking with him was nice.

She couldn't remember talking like this with any of the guys she'd dated. Keeping things light, meaningless—that had always been her motto. And she'd never had trouble sticking to it.

She sneaked a sideways glance at Alec. Black jacket, black gloves, black hat…and the bluest eyes she'd ever seen. Her heartbeat kicked up a notch.

"Not nuts. Courageous." The corners of his lips lifted, and those blue eyes glimmered like the stars overhead. "And spirited. Definitely spirited."

"I don't know about that." On the inside, though, she was smiling. Secretly she loved being thought of as spirited. "I mean, my father was a pilot. I grew up in the jump seat of his plane. Flying was never a question for me. It's a way of life."

"That's one way of looking at it. Not mine, though. I'll stick with spirited." He reached out and brushed a snowflake away from her eyes with a gentle swipe of his thumb.

Zoey found herself growing breathless, which she attributed to the thin mountain air. It couldn't be because Alec was standing so close. Close enough for her to see a tiny scar above his left eye that she'd never noticed before. Close enough to breathe in the scent of damp earth and evergreen trees coming from his parka.

Who are you, Alec Wynn? Who are you, really?

"I'm my father's daughter."

She wanted to share a part of herself she usually kept safely under wraps in hopes he might give her a glimpse of the man he was underneath all the hard edges. She didn't talk of her parents often. She told herself it was because they weren't really anyone's business, but the truth was that it still hurt. Even after all this time. "You know what they say—the apple doesn't fall far from the tree."

Alec grew very still.

And something changed. Zoey wasn't sure what, but the tender moment they'd shared suffered for it.

"That's what they say, all right." Icicles could have formed on his tongue. His tone was frostier than the Alaskan night. He shoved his hands in his pockets and looked down at her with thinly veiled revulsion in his gaze.

Nothing about their surroundings had altered. A herd of majestic reindeer still stood before them, and snow flurries still danced around them in a gentle waltz of winter beauty. But everything between them was different. Hard. Cold.

A shiver ran up and down Zoey's spine. She blinked up at him, bewildered at his sudden change of mood. "Alec…"

He took a step backward. "Good night, Zoey."

"Good night," she whispered, her words floating in a puff on the crisp arctic wind.

And then she could only watch wordlessly as he stepped farther away from her, with eyes as melancholy and blue as the bluest of Christmases, and retreated into the darkness.

Alec barged his way into the guest cabin, sat on the edge of his bed and dropped his head into his hands.

He hadn't seen it coming. Even when Zoey had started talking about her father and how she'd followed in his footsteps and become a pilot, he hadn't expected her to utter those words. He'd been caught off guard. Blindsided.

Hearing them come from Zoey's mouth had been a much-needed slap in the face. He wasn't angry with her. Far from it. He was grateful.

Because, until she'd said it, he'd been on the verge of kissing her.

Not that he would have actually gone through with it. But he'd thought about it. He'd thought about it a lot. Far more than he should have.

He wasn't even sure how it had happened. Sure, she was cute. More than cute, really. She was beautiful. The more time he spent with her, the more beautiful he found her. But it was that go-getter spirit of hers that really affected him. Even more so now that he knew about her past.

She was an orphan. An actual orphan. But instead of giving in to the role and being content to let people take care of her, she railed against it. For someone like Alec, who'd been struggling to overcome the past for most of his adult life, it was a quality to be respected.

And to top it off, she was a pilot. She climbed aboard an

airplane every day and soared into the same sky that had taken the lives of her family. That was the clincher right there. The moment she'd told him that, he knew he was a goner.

Until she'd said it. *The apple doesn't fall far from the tree.*

Fine. If that was how she felt, he was better off knowing it now…before he did something really stupid. Like give in to his urge to kiss her.

He would never have asked Camille to marry him if he'd thought she would believe such a thing. They'd met at church—the first church he'd ever attended. Walking into that building and hearing the message of how God could take a man and change him had been a life-altering experience. What was that verse again?

Therefore, if anyone is in Christ, he is a new creation; the old has gone, the new has come.

He still knew it by heart. How pathetic was that?

For a sweet, naïve time, he'd believed it. He'd believed it all. Then Camille's family had gotten involved. And in the end, they all thought he had the potential to become like his parents. Even Camille—the only person who'd ever had his back—had turned and run.

And a seed of doubt had taken root deep in Alec's consciousness. Maybe they were right.

Zoey apparently thought so.

He told himself he was being unreasonable. It was an expression. How was she to know how close it hit home for him?

Unreasonable or not, hearing her say it had been a wake-up call. Zoey was a good girl. As good as they came. She would never understand the things he'd seen and done. If she had the vaguest hint about his childhood, she'd probably consider him beyond redemption.

And she'd probably be right.

He shook his head, rubbed his face with his hands and eyed the deflated duffel bag tucked under the bureau in the corner. He could be packed and out the door in half an hour. He should just do it. Just leave and forget all about Alaska, all about Zoey and all about her reindeer.

As tempting as it was, he knew he couldn't do it. First, there was the practical matter of the money Zoey owed him. If he left now, he'd never see his thousand dollars. He had his doubts about recouping it, even if he did stay. More importantly, he'd given Zoey his word to stick around until Christmas. And no matter what anyone believed, Alec was a man of his word.

"Christmas it is," he muttered to himself as he stretched out on his back and rested his head on the pillow. But he'd made no promises about the New Year. He'd start looking on Craigslist first thing tomorrow. Maybe by the time Christmas rolled around, he could have something new lined up for January. And until then…

He sighed.

Until then he'd just have to remember that Zoey Hathaway was off-limits.

He let his eyes drift closed, and before he even realized what he was doing, he found himself talking to God.

Lord, I want to be a new creation. I'd love nothing more than to believe that the old has gone and the new has come. But I don't see how it's possible.

Help me be strong. Keep me from repeating the past. And keep me away from Zoey. She's a good person. She deserves better. Amen.

It was the first prayer he'd uttered in as long as he remembered.

Chapter Seven

Morning arrived early for Zoey, which was really saying something considering that, up until recently, she'd earned her living working at a coffee bar.

Sleep hadn't come easy. She'd felt like the lone guest at a slumber party. It had taken nearly half an hour to find her toothpaste, and when she finally did, it was in one of the kitchen drawers. She really hoped that had been a joke, either Clementine or Anya's doing, because who kept toothpaste by the kitchen sink?

In addition to feeling as though she was stumbling around someone else's home, she'd been plagued with thoughts of Alec and his odd behavior as they'd looked out over the reindeer. Just when she'd thought he might be the one person who'd ever really understood her, he'd shut her out. Was it something she'd said?

She'd turned their conversation over in her mind time and again as she'd lain in the dark, adjusting to all the sounds and scents of a new home. But she remained as mystified as ever. How could someone seem so soulful one minute and so distant the next?

She'd huffed in the darkness, pounded her pillow and pledged not to think about Alec anymore, but then memories of Gus crept in—the red flannel hat he'd worn every time she'd seen him in the cockpit of a plane, the way he'd always smelled of spearmint and black coffee, and his fondness for ice cream. Every year on her birthday since the death of her parents, Gus had taken her to Aurora's one and only ice-cream parlor and bought her the most extravagant sundae on the menu—a frosted chocolate-malt spectacular. Hot fudge, chocolate-malt ice cream, sticky marshmallow topping and malted milk balls, all served up in a frosty mug.

With two spoons.

Those memories, once so fond, were painful now. She didn't want to think about them. But alone in the dark, in Gus's home, she couldn't forget the way he'd always treated her like a granddaughter or how his wrinkled hands had begun to look increasingly fragile wrapped around the yoke of the Husky A-1C he piloted.

She'd scarcely slept. And it seemed as though her alarm sounded the moment her mind had finally stilled. The temptation to hit the snooze button ran deep. But she lived on a reindeer farm. Didn't that make her a farmer now? She supposed it did, even though in a matter of days she'd be a professional pilot. And didn't farmers rise at the crack of dawn?

She threw the covers off and dragged herself out of bed. Any thoughts of sleeping in were tempered by the snide comments she was sure to hear from Alec if she strolled outside after all the morning chores were done. Not that she had any real idea of what those morning chores might be.

After layering up in her thermals, parka and the warmest knit hat she owned, she headed for the door. But as her hand lingered on the knob, she spotted Gus's old flannel cap hanging on a peg on one of the knotty-pine walls. She smiled. She didn't think she could stand seeing it in the thrift store among so many discarded items. She was immensely thankful someone had realized the hat would carry sentimental value and chosen to leave it there. Anya's doing, most likely.

Impulsively, she tugged the woolen hat from her head and replaced it with Gus's flannel one. Her head might freeze, but wearing the cap was sure to warm her heart. And that was no small thing.

The snow was blowing hard, almost sideways. The reindeer didn't seem to mind, though. They were engaged in a boisterous game of chase, zipping across the pasture, kicking up snow in a flurry of hooves, sleek brown bodies and graceful antlers. The ground thundered beneath Zoey's feet, and she wondered how they managed not to slip and fall. She could see several icy patches from where she stood at the fence, but the reindeer floated over those areas with the same surefootedness as they did over the rest of the pasture. She envied them their grace and then made a mental note to check Google for more reindeer facts that might surprise her. Alec wasn't the only one who knew how to use a computer.

Where is he, anyway?

A peek in the barn proved rewarding. Alec was there, dressed in black, of course, shoveling hay into a wheelbarrow. His jacket strained across his broad back as he stabbed his shovel at the ground with more force than appeared necessary. A muscle flexed in his jaw, and the look on his face bordered on lethal.

Zoey's stomach fluttered. She'd dragged herself out of bed to face this? She was tempted to climb back under the covers.

"Good morning," she chirped. She sounded absurdly cheerful for this early hour, even to herself.

Alec cast a dismissive glance over his shoulder and said nothing.

She plowed on. "So, tell me what I can do to help."

He shrugged. "Most everything's already done."

"And I thought I'd gotten up early. You must have risen

with the sun." What little sun there was at this time of year in Alaska. The violet haze hanging over the horizon was the closest thing to a sunrise they would see in a snowfall like this one.

"Couldn't sleep," he grumbled.

"I guess I'll go on back to bed, then." She crossed her arms and waited for the spoiled-princess comment that was sure to follow.

Nothing.

He must really be in a bad way, she thought.

"Come on. I want to pitch in. Surely there's something I can do."

He let out a huff and jammed his shovel into the frozen earth. "Zoey..."

"Alec." She mimicked his grumpy tone.

The subtlest of smiles tipped his lips, and Zoey's breath hitched in her throat. A sullen man had never looked so handsome. "I've got things under control. You're paying me to work here, remember?"

Zoey made a face. "Not technically. Gus paid you for the month, remember?"

"Regardless, I've been paid. You can go about your business." He glanced at her snow boots with a glimmer of amusement in his eyes. "Don't your toenails need painting or something?"

"Done." She crossed her arms. Her toenails were still only halfway painted as a result of her mad dash from her pedicure the other day, but he didn't need to know that. "And my tiara is all polished, too."

He shook his head and looked at her for a long, silent moment as if weighing his options. "If you really want to do something..."

"I do."

He let out a tortured sigh. "Fine."

She grinned in triumph.

"I wouldn't look so excited if I were you. What we…er, the reindeer…really need is hay."

"Hay. Got it." She looked around. What little hay she could see was all piled in the wheelbarrow. It looked like a paltry amount for thirty-one reindeer, even to someone who had no clue what they did with it. "This is all there is?"

"Unfortunately, yes."

He didn't utter a word about money. He didn't have to. Zoey was beginning to see dollar signs everywhere she turned.

It was hay. How much could it possibly cost? "Where do we get more?"

"This time of year, you'll probably have to get someone to fly it in. Last time I checked, there was a pile of it stored in a hangar in Anchorage. It's not going to be cheap." His gaze shifted away from her, and she got the feeling he'd been avoiding talking to her about this particular matter.

Her thoughts toward him warmed once again. He'd wanted to spare her more bad news. He might not want to admit it, or even act like it, but he cared.

A goofy smile made its way to her lips before she could stop it. "Aren't you forgetting something? I'm a pilot."

"Aren't *you* forgetting something?" He crossed his arms. "You don't have a plane."

"I'm sure someone will let me borrow one." She shrugged.

Truth be told, getting her hands on an airplane with less than a day's notice would be complicated at best. Complicated, but not impossible.

"Of course they will." Alec rolled his eyes. "I should have known."

"You're coming with me, right?"

"Where?" He narrowed his gaze at her.

"To get the hay." She waved a hand around the empty barn.

"You said things were under control here, didn't you? So you can come along. You can be my copilot."

He paled a little.

And to Zoey's complete and utter astonishment, he looked somewhat squeamish.

"You're not scared, are you?" she asked, relishing the moment far more than she should have.

"Of course not," he snapped. "Don't be ridiculous."

"My mistake." She winked at him and earned nothing more than a scowl in return.

And she knew without a doubt she'd hit the nail right on the head. "I'll make some calls and see what I can arrange. With any luck we'll be wheels up by noon."

"Can't wait," he said through a smile as fake as the beard on a department-store Santa.

Zoey had to bite her lip to keep from laughing out loud as she walked back toward the house. For the first time since she'd met Alec, she had the upper hand.

At last. It was about time. Because he could deny it all he wanted, but she'd seen that look of trepidation on the faces of enough passengers to know exactly what it meant.

Alec Wynn—Mr. Tough Guy, the same man who'd ridden a Harley from Washington State to Alaska in the dead of winter—was afraid of flying.

The plane that Zoey somehow managed to procure was a Cessna 185, which meant nothing to Alec. But Zoey assured him it was good news. As far as bush planes in Alaska went, it was one of the roomier models.

Alec began to suspect she was pulling his leg when he was forced to fold himself in half to fit in the seat beside hers. "If this is one of the more comfortable planes, I'd hate to see the alternative."

"Quit complaining. You have oodles of room." Zoey

flipped a page on the clipboard in her lap, turning to what appeared to be some sort of checklist.

"*Oodles?* Is that a technical term?"

"Yes. All the pilots use it." She turned to face him. On any given day, Zoey's skin had a radiant quality that was difficult, if not impossible, to overlook. But sitting at the controls of that airplane, her cheeks glowed, pinker and more lovely than Alec had ever seen them. Clearly, she was in her element. "Are you all buckled in?"

Too bad her element felt like a near-death experience to Alec. And they'd yet to leave the ground. "Yes, captain."

She reached over and gave his seat belt a yank.

His pulse kicked up a notch at her touch. He told himself it was merely a product of the adrenaline rushing through his system, and he almost believed it. "Ouch."

"Sorry. I had to make sure. It's on the list." She motioned toward her preflight checklist anchored on the clipboard in her lap as she pulled away.

Not far enough.

That was the trouble with this tin can of a plane. There was no personal space. His plan to stay far away from Zoey was a literal impossibility.

Her enthusiasm, that irrepressible spirit that was so uniquely Zoey, rolled off her in waves. He couldn't help but get caught up in it. Despite the nerves skittering through him, he was anxious to get airborne and see the world the way she preferred to see it. Even worse, he could smell her perfume. Something warm and sweet…sandalwood, maybe? No. Vanilla. Definitely vanilla.

He'd known this was a bad idea.

"Alec," she said as the plane's engine roared to life. "Try to relax, for once in your life."

Relax.

He was a little too relaxed for his liking. Zoey already had the greater population of Aurora wrapped around her finger, and if he wasn't careful, he wouldn't be too far behind.

"Put these on." She handed him a pair of headphones similar to the ones she was already wearing.

He did as she said, and in an instant the roar of the engine dulled to a soft purr.

"Better?" Her voice was crisp and clear. It vibrated through his chest.

"Yes." He'd never thought of flying with someone as a particularly intimate experience, but this felt like it.

He fixed his gaze on the horizon. Easy, because they were surrounded by windows on all sides. The heavy snowfall of the morning had slowed, leaving just a hint of flurries swirling through the air. The Chugach Mountains rose before them, jagged and white, like something carved out of ivory. Anchorage, and a few bales of hay, lay on the other side.

So did the afternoon mail delivery for Aurora, apparently. In exchange for the use of his plane, Zoey had agreed to make the mail run for the local pilot who contracted with the postal service. Since his wife was in the hospital, he'd readily agreed. Zoey knew all about the situation—and now Alec did, too—because people in Aurora obviously knew everything there was to know about everyone else.

Zoey said some things to the tower, and the plane crawled forward. Alec probably would have gripped the armrests, if there had been any.

They gained speed more slowly than he would have expected. He felt the plane's skis skid a fraction on the ice-covered lake. Zoey didn't appear concerned, though. She made some small adjustments to the yoke, and the wings on either side of them evened out. Before it felt as if they were going fast enough to pull onto a state highway, Alec felt the ground fall from beneath them.

And then they were floating, like one of the snowflakes.

The plane lifted higher and higher until they were soaring far above the ring of evergreens that surrounded the lake and heading into the blue mist of the distance. Alec's breath caught in his throat. It was incredible. Like riding his motorcycle, only better. No wonder she loved it so much.

"See?" Zoey cast him a sideways glance. She had a smile on her face as big as the one gathering inside him. "I told you this wasn't so different from flying in a big jet."

"I wouldn't actually know," he said quietly into his headset.

Zoey's head snapped in his direction. "What?"

"I've never flown before...big jet, ski plane or otherwise." He wasn't sure what prompted him to say it. He could have just nodded in agreement rather than letting go of any personal information.

But it didn't seem right. Not here, not now.

They were a world away from Aurora. He could barely see the sleepy town below them anymore.

Zoey reached out and touched his arm, dragging his attention away from the view and back toward her. He found her looking at him with a painful mixture of curiosity and hurt on her face. "Why didn't you tell me?"

He swallowed. "It didn't seem important."

"You know an awful lot about me, Alec. And I know nothing about you."

And that was just the way he preferred it. "What do you want to know?"

"Everything." She grinned. "Tell me everything."

His expression hardened. She had no idea what she was asking. "We don't have that kind of time. Isn't Anchorage less than an hour away?"

"True. Then tell me *one* thing about yourself, mystery man. Not something silly, like your favorite color, because I'm pretty sure it's black." She rolled her eyes.

"One thing?"

"Yes. Something real." She turned to him again with a look of hopeful expectation shining in her eyes that reached right toward Alec and grabbed him by the throat.

And he couldn't just ignore it…that look. He tried. He really did. He kept his gaze fixed on the front window of the plane, staring out at the mountains, the clouds, the elusive rays of the sun hiding behind the gray. And still all he could see was that look. She wanted something from him. Nothing huge, just a tiny piece of him.

And despite himself, he wanted to give it to her. As the plane's wings seemed to graze an endless cluster of evergreens, he said, "I've never had a Christmas tree. I didn't have what you'd call a traditional upbringing."

The words slid right out of him, as if he'd been waiting to tell someone since the day he'd first set foot in Alaska. Not just someone…

Her.

"Normal things, like vacations, flying, Christmas trees, weren't exactly part of the picture," he added.

"I see," she said.

But she didn't. Not really. Because he hadn't actually told her anything. Not yet.

"I come from a bad place. My parents were…are…addicts." He released a long-overdue breath. "So, there. That's your one thing."

She said nothing at first, not that Alec could blame her. He'd probably given her a lot more than she'd bargained for. But at least it was out in the open. She might not know all the details, but she knew more than he'd ever shared with anyone else.

Zoey's voice went quiet. Soft. "How long has it been since you've seen your family?"

"Not since I was a teenager. A very long time." But that

wasn't altogether true, was it? "My dad turned up out of the blue recently, asking for money. That's why I left Washington. I want all that behind me, once and for all."

As if such a thing were remotely possible.

"I'm glad you did." She slid her gaze toward him, her eyes greener and more vibrant than an entire field of evergreen trees.

Looking into that sea of green, Alec thought all the aching memories of his past seemed far away. Further than the ground that swirled beneath them now, little more than misty hints of snow-covered peaks, barely discernible through the heavy layer of soft white clouds. The time he'd spent thus far with Zoey stood out from all the pain he'd experienced as something else entirely. Something sweet and pure. As exasperating as he sometimes found her, she had a lightness about her that drew him in. Soothed him.

"I have another question," she said.

There was that exasperating quality again.

Alec sighed. "You asked me to tell you one thing. Mission accomplished."

"This question is related, so it really doesn't count."

He felt a grin sneak its way to his lips. Why on earth was he smiling? "I'll be the judge of that."

"You said you've never had a Christmas tree. Given your childhood, I understand. But what about since you've been an adult? Have you really never had a tree? Never ever?" She sounded flabbergasted, as if he'd told her the moon was made of cheese. Or that reindeer could really fly.

"Never ever," he echoed. The words sounded far less whimsical coming from his own mouth.

"Why not?"

She'd moved so far beyond a single question that he'd lost count. "I almost had a Christmas tree. Once."

"What happened?" She turned those big doe eyes on him again, and he knew there was no denying her.

He may as well just say it—just spill his guts and get it over with. "A few Christmases ago, I was engaged to be married. I went out and bought a Christmas tree, our first. The first of many, or so I thought. It turned out to be the end. She broke things off before I could even take it off the roof of the car."

There was a prolonged pause, then Zoey whispered, "Why?"

Alec would have liked to think it was a complicated question with a complicated answer, that engagements didn't just end. But they did. His had, hadn't it? In an instant, his future had become just as bleak as his past. "She realized that, given where I'd come from, I could never be the kind of man she needed. She was probably right. It was for the best. There, now you know as much about me as I know about you. I think that makes us even."

Even—with the minor exception of the thousand dollars she still owed him. Funny, he'd begun to think about that less and less.

The silence in his headphones was deafening. About the time that Alec began to wonder if they were still turned on, if Zoey had actually heard anything he'd said, she responded with two simple words. "Thank you."

Then her right hand released its hold on the yoke and found his, her petal-soft skin sliding against his rough, calloused fingers as their hands intertwined.

Alec knew it was wrong. He might have told her about his family, his fiancée, but that didn't mean he was the man for her. He wasn't. She'd been through enough in her brief, painful life. He wasn't about to add his staggering levels of dysfunction into the mix.

Let go.

He didn't.

What was wrong with him? If he couldn't—or wouldn't—let go, he needed to do something to bring some levity to the situation. To get things back to a state that vaguely resembled normal. As normal as things could be, given that they were soaring high above the mountains. The scenery out the window was growing hazy, as if Aurora were nothing more than an afterthought.

But it wasn't. Alec knew better.

The world was spread out below them in a swirl of greens, blues and snowy white. It was as painfully real as ever. He'd never been able to outrun the real world before. Why would now be any different?

He glanced over at Zoey sitting beside him. Her eyes glowed like the brightest of Christmas lights, and her hair tumbled over her shoulders in thick, golden waves from a simple, worn plaid hat perched on her head. It was a flat cap. Flannel. And it looked like something an old man would have worn—twenty or thirty years ago, if the fraying flannel on the edges was any indication.

Except there was no denying the fact that Zoey was no old man.

"Nice hat," he said, tongue planted firmly in cheek.

She slid him a dubious glance. "Are you making fun of my hat?"

"Not at all." He bit back a smile. "You look like a ninety-year-old man. That's the look you're going for, right?"

"Absolutely." She beamed at him as if he'd told her she was the most beautiful girl in the world.

The old has gone, the new has come.

Those remembered words of promise hit him hard, straight in the chest.

Alec had difficulty swallowing, or even breathing, for a moment. When he managed to get himself together, he dropped his gaze to the fir trees dotting the landscape below. He focused all his concentration on the snow blowing across the tundra like a sandstorm and the massive chunks of ice breaking free from Alaska's shore and floating out to sea. Those things were real. Those things he could see and touch. Not like whatever fleeting moment of infatuation he was currently experiencing.

Not like any of God's promises he'd believed in so long ago.

And ever so slowly, he loosened his fingers and released Zoey's hand.

Chapter Eight

Alec paused from dishing out reindeer pellets the next morning and glanced at the display of his ringing cell phone. The number was unfamiliar but bore the Alaskan area code. "Hello?"

"I think I've found something."

Alec took a wild guess. "Brock?"

"Yeah, it's me," he said. Alec could hear dogs barking in the background. Lots of dogs, from the sound of things. "I think I've found you a dog."

"You're kidding." Alec tossed a final scoopful of pellets into the feed bin and watched as the reindeer made short work of their breakfast.

It had been only two days since he'd mentioned the dog idea to Brock. He couldn't have already located one, could he?

"Nope. I'm dead serious. Some of the search-and-rescue breeders I work with pointed me in the right direction. And believe it or not, the dog is here in Alaska." There was more barking in the background. Alec hoped all that racket wasn't coming from the reindeer dog. "We can go pick her up today if you're free."

Alec glanced across the pasture toward the house. He was pretty sure Zoey had left sometime during the early-morning hours. The windows were dark, and the driveway was empty. He had no clue where she'd gone, which was fine. He wasn't her keeper.

And she wasn't his. He'd give her a call and let her know he was stepping out for a while, just out of courtesy. Or better yet, leave a note.

"Sounds good," he said. "I could probably get away in about an hour or so."

"The dog is in Knik, about an hour's drive from here. The breeder's been training her to herd muskoxen. Hopefully, the reindeer will be an easy transition. We can head on up there in my truck." That solved the problem of how to give a dog a ride on Alec's motorcycle. "Can you meet me at the Northern Lights Inn coffee bar?"

"Sure. See you there."

Alec shoved his cell phone back in his pocket. Coffee sounded good. Very good. He hadn't exactly gotten a good night's rest the night before. The exchange with Zoey in the airplane had left him edgy and unable to sleep. Even though the rest of the day had been perfectly ordinary and uneventful, that brief moment they'd shared nagged at him. There was certainly nothing dreamy or romantic about riding back from Anchorage with half a dozen bales of hay pressed into his back. But the ride up there had been extraordinary. He wasn't sure whether to blame the scenery or the company, but for a minute there he'd remembered what it felt like to hope. To believe in the possibility that things could be different.

He didn't want to remember what that was like. He'd been doing just fine on his own. So it was probably a good thing he'd be gone for a large part of the day. Just in case. A little time and space couldn't hurt.

He finished up around the ranch, scrawled a note for Zoey and made it to the coffee bar with a minute or two to spare. Brock hadn't arrived yet, so Alec unwound his scarf and shrugged out of his parka. He'd just sat down when his gaze snagged on a jar on the counter stuffed with dollar bills.

The jar was decorated with plastic googly eyes, twig antlers and a red, fuzzy pompom nose.

"Rudolph?" Alec groaned. "Really?"

And if that wasn't cutesy—and annoying—enough, a wraparound label at the bottom of the jar urged contributors to Save the Reindeer!

Save the reindeer?

Bewildered, Alec picked up the jar and searched it for further information. None was forthcoming. Then as he sat there staring into Rudolph's googly eyes, mortification settled in his gut.

Save the reindeer!

The whole thing had Zoey's name written all over it.

So this was her grand plan of how she was going to pay him what she owed him? A kitschy little donation jar with twig antlers? What was next? Was she going to force Palmer to stand on the street corner with jingle bells around his neck and a red kettle, Salvation Army–style?

He blanched at the thought. Just when he'd come to terms with working on a reindeer farm, she'd gone and cranked things into saccharine Yuletide overdrive.

He peered into the jar. There were at least ten ones shoved inside, along with a five. Fifteen dollars.

Only nine hundred eighty-five to go.

"Can I help you?" the barista asked, giving him a suspicious once-over.

He replaced the jar and slid it away from him with a push of his pointer finger. Not that he didn't have every right to fish the five out of there and use it to buy an espresso or something.

"Coffee. Black, please."

Satisfied that he wasn't about to steal from the reindeer

who apparently needed saving, the barista aimed a megawatt smile at him. "Are you sure you wouldn't like to try an iced gingerbread latte? Or a peppermint hot chocolate?"

Did he look like one of Santa's elves or something? "No, thanks. Just the coffee."

"Here you go." She handed him a steaming mug. "It's our special holiday blend."

Of course it is. "Thanks."

He took a sip. Holiday blend notwithstanding, it hit the spot. He took another swig, and an eerie feeling came over him, as though someone were watching him.

He lowered his coffee cup. The round plastic eyes on the mason reindeer jar bored into him. Alec scowled and turned it so it faced the other direction.

"Alec—hey, man." Brock sauntered up to the coffee bar and slapped him on the back.

"Morning," Alec said.

"I see the Save the Reindeer project has gotten off the ground." Brock spun the jar back around.

"You knew about this?" Alec asked.

Brock snorted. "You didn't?"

"The ranch hand is always the last to know." Alec rolled his eyes.

"The girls got together early this morning and made dozens of these things."

So that was where Zoey had gone. "Dozens?" Alec winced.

"They're all over town," Brock said and took a to-go cup from the barista.

Alec finished off the last of his coffee and shook his head. All over town? He had to hand it to her—when she had a plan, she committed to it 100 percent.

A single adjective danced in his consciousness.

Spunky.

His heart gave a rebellious surge.

"You ready to head out of town?" Brock asked, tearing him from his thoughts.

Distance. That was what Alec needed. He needed it in spades. "Couldn't be readier."

Zoey took a deep breath and strode toward the administration office at the airport armed with one of her googly-eyed reindeer jars. Her gaze lingered on the coffee bar, visible through the big picture windows that lined the back entrance of the Northern Lights Inn. She thought she might spot Alec inside since she'd seen his motorcycle parked out front, but the barstools were empty.

Interesting.

She wondered where he was. Then she chastised herself for wondering.

She shouldn't care. Shouldn't and didn't. The only thing that mattered was that the reindeer were taken care of. She didn't even need to think twice about their welfare. Alec had proven himself trustworthy in that regard, time and again. She could still hardly wrap her mind around the fact that he'd stuck around and tended to them after Gus had died. How long would he have stayed if she'd never shown up? A month? Two?

Forever?

Zoey shook off the thought. Alec might be devoted to the reindeer, but she had the distinct feeling that *forever* wasn't part of his vocabulary. Maybe it was all the black. Or maybe it was the motorcycle.

Maybe it's the way he always freezes up the minute the conversation turns personal.

She frowned as she remembered what he'd told her in the plane on the way to Anchorage.

I come from a bad place.

I was engaged... I could never be the kind of man she needed.

She'd wanted to get to know him, but she'd had no idea what she would find once he began to open up. He could have told her anything, but he'd picked something utterly private. And heartbreaking.

And then he'd retreated back into his shell.

Why did he even tell her, if he'd rather pretend he hadn't? Had he simply been making conversation? Had she misinterpreted that soulful look he'd given her—the one that made her feel less alone than she'd felt in as long as she could remember? He'd held her hand.

And she'd thought…

She squeezed her eyes shut.

Never mind what she'd thought. She wasn't here looking for Alec. She was here to plead her case with Chuck about the FAA fine.

A nervous flutter ran through her. She could do this. She could totally do this. But she might need to visit her plane first, to muster up some courage.

She gripped the reindeer jar tighter, being careful not to accidentally break one of the antlers as she bypassed the office doors and headed toward the lake. The snow was ankle-deep, and it would have been impossible to discern where the beach ended and the lake began if not for the ring of ski planes dotting the shoreline. Hers was the fourth in line, and her breath hitched in her throat when she spotted it.

There she is, Zoey thought. *My baby.*

The plane was yellow and black, as vivid as a bumblebee. If it wasn't the most beautiful thing Zoey had ever seen, then it was close. And it would be all hers in just a matter of days.

God willing.

She stood and admired the way the muted sunlight glinted off its windows. If she stood in precisely the right spot, her reflection made it look as though she were sitting in the cockpit. *Someday soon,* she mused, and she tucked the reindeer jar under her arm as she brushed away a layer of snow that had piled up on the wing closest to her. She knew it was silly, but she didn't like seeing her plane buried like that. It looked lonely.

Once the bright yellow wings were cleared of snow—and her mittens soaked—she turned around and headed back toward the airport offices. Pearl, the receptionist, greeted Zoey with a smile as she pushed through the glass door and stomped the snow from her boots.

"Morning, Zoey," Pearl said. "Are you here on business, or is another one of your reindeer here for a visit?"

Zoey grimaced. Every one of Alaska's estimated one hundred thousand glaciers would melt sooner than she would live down the Palmer incident. "Business. Is Chuck available, or is he up in the tower?"

"He's around here somewhere. Let me page him for you." Pearl picked up the phone, and Chuck's name was echoing through the small building.

To Zoey's relief, he soon appeared, coffee cup in hand. "Zoey, good to see you. Is today the big day?" He nodded toward the window. Her airplane now looked clean and well cared for.

Zoey's stomach did a little flip-flop. The closing day on the purchase of her plane had once seemed so far down the road. Now it was looming closer and closer. "Not yet. Friday."

"Friday." He nodded. "Well, good for you."

He looked as though he meant it, which hadn't always been the case.

When Zoey had first begun investigating flying lessons, she'd had trouble finding an instructor. Not that she didn't know any teaching pilots—on the contrary, she knew plenty. All of her dad's friends were still flying. She'd been sure one of them would be happy to take her on as a student. Truth be told, she'd actually thought they'd *all* be happy to take her into their fold.

Not so. No one wanted to teach her how to fly a plane. She was certain it had something to do with her parents' deaths but wasn't sure about the specifics. Maybe they thought she'd freak out once she got up there. Who knew? But no amount of begging or cajoling landed her an instructor.

Until she'd approached Gus Henderson.

Her throat tightened at the memory of him. She owed him so much.

"I was hoping we could have a word about the FAA fine," she said in as confident a tone as she could muster.

Chuck's smile dimmed somewhat. "Yes, that. Come on into my office."

She followed him down the hall, her heart beating quicker with each step. She tried to calm herself down by focusing on the scenic photographs lining the walls—a shiny red biplane swooping over evergreen-covered hilltops, a full moon hanging low over pink Alaskan mountains at dusk. It was no use. By the time Chuck escorted her into his office, she felt as though she might faint.

Everything depended on this moment.

Lord, please.

She wasn't praying so much as begging. Desperate times called for desperate measures. "About the fine..." she started.

Chuck exhaled a weary sigh.

Zoey felt bad continuing, but she didn't have much of a choice. "When exactly is it due?"

"Immediately."

Panic beat in frantic wings against her rib cage. "Um, how immediate is immediate?"

"Zoey." Chuck leaned back in his chair. "You know I'd do anything to help you out, but my hands are tied. We're talking about the federal government here. The FAA isn't known for its flexibility. One of the conditions of the reduced fine is that it will be paid within ten days."

"Ten days." She gulped.

"Well, eight now. Another two days have passed."

She sat perfectly still, trying to digest this information. She'd hoped she would have until the New Year to come up with the two thousand dollars she owed the FAA for Palmer's little romp. She'd written a three-figure check the day before for the hay the reindeer needed. If she wrote another check right now for the FAA fine, she would be short for the down payment on the airplane. It was time for plan B....

Except there *was* no plan B.

She stared down at the googly-eyed reindeer jar in her hands, the closest thing to a plan B that she had at the moment.

"That's cute," Chuck said, following her gaze. "What is it, exactly?"

"It's a donation jar. Part of my plan to save the reindeer farm." She forced a smile. Things couldn't be as bad as they seemed. They just couldn't. "I was hoping I could leave one out in the reception area."

"Of course." He nodded. "Of course. You know we're all on your side, Zoey. All of us. The whole town."

The whole town was on her side. But was it enough?

"Excuse me." Pearl popped her head inside the door. "I hate to interrupt, but there's been an emergency of sorts."

Chuck pushed out of his chair. "An emergency?"

"Sorry." Pearl winced. "Not an airport emergency. A reindeer emergency."

All eyes swiveled toward Zoey.

Not again. Seriously. This was getting beyond the scope of what any sane person could deal with. "Palmer isn't in the middle of the runway again, is he?"

"No." Pearl shook her head. "It's not that."

Relief zinged through Zoey. No new FAA fines! "What's he gotten into this time? He's not holding up traffic on Main Street or anything, is he?"

"Actually, he *is* on Main Street." Pearl pulled a face.

Zoey stood, zipped up her parka and wished she'd thought to stuff her pockets with carrots before she'd left the house. She was probably going to have to start carrying them around with her wherever she went, which was just sad. Not to mention a little weird. "I'll go round him up. Do you have any idea where on Main Street he's camped out?"

"The courthouse." Pearl nodded, but the worried glance she sent Chuck gave Zoey pause.

How bad could it be? At least he wasn't holding up air traffic this time. "Pearl, what are you not telling me?"

"It seems Palmer has had a bit of an altercation."

Zoey froze with one of her mittens halfway in place. Surely Palmer hadn't hurt anyone. Alec had promised he wasn't dangerous. "Altercation? With who?"

"With a few other reindeer," Pearl said.

Zoey groaned. "Just how many of my reindeer escaped?"

"Oh, don't worry, dear." Pearl gave Zoey's shoulder a squeeze. "Just the one. Just Palmer. But it seems he's a little confused."

He wasn't the only one. "Confused? How?"

"It seems he thinks the wooden reindeer that are part of the courthouse Christmas display are real." Pearl offered a sympathetic smile. "And he's attacking them."

A staccato burst of laughter erupted from Chuck.

Zoey wanted to cry. "Okay, I can handle this. I can totally handle this."

She wasn't sure who she was trying to convince—Pearl and Chuck, or herself. Either way, she finished tugging on her mittens and readied herself to collect her macho-yet-woefully-disoriented reindeer.

If Palmer's airport escapade had made the evening news, she hated to think what kind of coverage this latest antic would get. She clamped her eyes shut, fighting against the image of a bloodthirsty Palmer head-butting a fake reindeer on the front page of the *Yukon Reporter.* She could forget being known as the town orphan. Thanks to Palmer, she'd ventured into town-laughingstock territory.

I can do this. She forced her eyes open.

Just as she was about to leave, she remembered the donation jar. She handed it to Pearl. "Here. This is for the reception area."

Pearl turned it over in her hand, and the googly eyes rolled around and around. "Save the Reindeer? Which ones? Yours, or the poor victims down at the courthouse?" She released a snort of laughter.

"Funny," Zoey said with a shaky smile.

"I thought so," Chuck said, laughing with even more gusto. So much so that his belly shook, not unlike a bowl full of jelly.

"Thank you for your help. Chuck, I'll have a check on your desk by end of day tomorrow." She heard more laughter from Chuck's office as she made her way out of the building.

Was it crazy to think she could collect two thousand dollars in the donation jars by then? Surely it was no crazier than a reindeer attacking a Christmas display. That thought brought little comfort, however.

She bent her head against the wind as she strode away from the airport and toward her car. A solitary tear slipped down her cheek. She batted it away with a swipe of her mitten.

Lord, I'm not sure I can do this.

Chapter Nine

The dog looked like a bear. A fuzzy, brown bear with a curled tail, pricked ears and a coat so profuse that Alec wasn't completely sure where all that fur ended and her body began. As they drove back to Aurora from Knik in Brock's truck, puffs of chocolate-colored dog hair drifted through the air, propelled by the force of the heater.

"She won't shed like this once we get to Zoey's place," Brock said. "She's probably nervous, wondering where she's headed. And she needs that thick double coat for working outdoors."

"What breed is she, again? In case Zoey asks." He wanted to be able to accurately describe the animal he was bringing home. Now that his idea had become a living, breathing dog, seeds of doubt had begun to take root.

He was giving her a dog.

Did she even like dogs? He couldn't imagine she didn't. Dogs were sweet. And fluffy, this one in particular. And Zoey seemed like the type of girl—*woman,* his consciousness screamed—who appreciated all things sweet and fluffy.

But what kind of message was he sending her, giving her a dog?

He couldn't worry about that now. The deed was done.

He'd forked over several hundred dollars for the thing and sworn Brock to secrecy as to exactly how much she'd cost. And now she sat in the truck directly behind him, breathing hot air on the back of his neck.

"She's a Finnish Lapphund, a true reindeer-herding breed." Brock shook his head in wonder as he steered the truck into the Northern Lights Inn parking lot and pulled alongside Alec's motorcycle. "A real find. They're not all that common."

"And this isn't Finland," Alec added dryly.

"Nope." Brock laughed. "It's not."

Finland, Alaska—what difference did it make? Reindeer were reindeer. And the breeder had shown Alec and Brock what the dog could do with a herd of muskoxen. It had been extraordinary. Surely she could keep Palmer in check.

Alec paused with his hand on the door handle. "Listen, I want to thank you for all your help with this. I think it will mean a lot to Zoey."

Brock nodded. "No problem. Zoey's a good friend. I'd do anything for a friend, you included."

He slapped Alec on the back.

Alec made every effort not to flinch. He wasn't good with touching. It wasn't any mystery as to why, and it rarely came up since he kept mostly to himself. Brock was a good guy. Alec could tell.

Still, edginess crept under Alec's skin. He was going to have to say something about the forest and how their time there had overlapped. Even though the last thing he wanted to discuss was his past—any part of it—keeping it a secret no longer seemed right. "You know, we've met before. I'm not sure if you remember."

"Sure I do." The dog poked her head between the driver and passenger seats, and Brock gave her a hearty scratch between the ears. "Washington. Olympic Forest."

Alec nodded, unsure how to continue. Just how much did Brock remember about that day? "You found that boy."

Brock shook his head. "My dog found that boy. I was just the one on the other end of the leash."

"Either way, it was impressive."

"Well, hopefully your new dog will be equally hardworking." Brock grinned.

"Not my dog. Zoey's." He and Zoey weren't a unit, a couple. They were two separate people, and they always would be.

"Zoey's dog. Right." Brock glanced at the dog again. "How are we going to do this? You still want to surprise her?"

Alec's seeds of doubt sprouted into a blooming garden. He hoped this wasn't a huge mistake. Otherwise, he'd be stuck with a dog that herded muskoxen. Just what he needed. "Do you mind giving the dog a ride back to the farm? I'll meet you there on my bike."

"Sounds good. See you in a few." Brock waved and shifted the truck back into Drive.

As Alec pulled on his helmet and climbed onto his motorcycle, he breathed a tentative sigh of relief. Brock either didn't remember the episode with his father at the park-ranger's office, or he knew not to bring it up. Superb. It was difficult enough not to dwell on the past, not to succumb to the fear that one day he would turn into his parents, without constant reminders.

It was a sobering thought—that he might have something sick and twisted lurking inside him, waiting for some unknown moment to rise to the surface. This was his deepest fear, the thing that kept him up at night.

The thing that kept him away from Zoey Hathaway.

He tightened the chin strap of his helmet. Right now he had more pressing things to worry about than his faulty genetics, like introducing Zoey to her new dog.

Brock bid him good luck as he helped unload the dog and

left Alec standing in the farm's frozen driveway, holding the dog's leash in one hand and a giant bag of kibble under his arm.

While Brock's truck disappeared from view, Alec scanned the horizon. Reindeer dotted the pasture in groups of twos and threes, some trotting and tossing their heads, others resting against the fence with their legs tucked beneath them. Only one stood alone—Palmer, with his head bowed and eyes downcast. At first glance, Alec thought he was grazing, but his mouth wasn't moving. He was simply standing there.

Alec frowned. It was kind of sad seeing him on his own like that. But at least he was here and not off somewhere causing trouble. And if he was depressed, that was where the dog might come in handy.

"It's now or never," Alec muttered and glanced down at the dog. She looked ordinary in every way. Then again, Brock's dogs looked like regular pets, too. "You ready?"

The dog's mouth stretched open in a wide yawn.

"Your enthusiasm is overwhelming." He chuckled. "Come on. Let's introduce you to your new owner."

He led the dog to the front porch and knocked twice on the door to the cabin. After several seconds with no response, his gut churned with worry. Zoey's car was parked in the drive. Why wasn't she answering?

He knocked again, with more force this time.

Still no answer.

He huffed out a breath.

"You." He looked down at the dog. "Stay here."

Then he tried the knob. It turned easily. Alec's teeth clenched. Of course she hadn't locked the door. Anyone could have walked right in.

He would lecture her about that later. First, he needed to find her and make sure she was safe.

"Zoey?" he called into the dimly lit living room.

"Over here."

He barely heard her response. It was little more than a whisper. Relief, mixed with a heavy dose of irritation, shot through him at the sound of it.

He stalked into the living room and found her sitting at the kitchen table, as calm as could be. "I've been standing out there pounding on your door."

"Sorry," she said, as if in a daze, and lifted one of her delicate shoulders.

"I was worried something had happened to you." He jammed his hands on his hips and tried to calm his breathing as the memory of Gus Henderson's lifeless body struck him fast and hard. "And your door was wide open. Anyone could have walked right in."

She snapped out of her daze and lifted an angry eyebrow. "Someone did."

"You know good and well what I mean. You could have been hurt." He inhaled a ragged breath. "I thought I was going to walk in here and find you injured…or worse."

Her gaze softened, and her eyes changed from steely emeralds to a tranquil sea green. "You were really worried about me, weren't you?"

"Can you blame me?" He crossed his arms and did his best to stay annoyed. Those eyes of hers somehow reached right inside him and smoothed away the sharp edges of his anger, leaving something far more dangerous in its place. Something he didn't want to feel—something that felt an awful lot like attraction.

He didn't want to be attracted to her. He didn't even want to be worried about her. Why did she make him so crazy?

"This is about Gus, isn't it?" She stood and rested a hand on his arm.

"Yes. And no." He took a step backward, out of her reach. Hurt flashed in her eyes for the briefest of moments, and then her lips fell into a flat, stubborn line again. *Stop looking at her lips.* "Just lock your doors, would you? You're too trusting of people."

"You're not the boss of me. The last time I checked, it was the other way around." She pinned him with a glare. "Besides, I know everyone within a hundred-mile radius. You're the only stranger around here. Are you telling me I shouldn't trust *you?*"

"Maybe I am, sweetheart," he said, his voice tinged with a sadness he couldn't hide.

She looked at him for a long, silent beat, until her gaze came to rest on the scar above his eye—the one his father had put there on Alec's tenth birthday.

He raked a hand through his hair, hiding the scar from view in the process.

Zoey sighed. "I'm sorry if I worried you. I wasn't up to facing anyone, least of all you."

Just what was that supposed to mean?

Before he could ask, she scooped a stack of papers off the table and thrust them at his chest. "Here. Take a look. I'm surprised you haven't already heard."

He glanced down at the slim yellow pages. They looked like traffic tickets.

"Criminal mischief?" He suppressed a snicker. He really couldn't see Zoey causing any trouble, least of all criminal. "Destruction of government property?" He raised his brows.

Zoey crossed her arms. "Keep reading. There's one more."

"Animal at large." Alec's jaw hardened. *Palmer.* He looked back up at Zoey. "What did he do this time?"

"Don't laugh." She poked him hard in the chest. "If you so much as giggle, I will fire you on the spot."

"Who's laughing?" He tossed the citations on the table and planted his hands on his hips. "And I never giggle. Ever."

She let out a long, measured breath before speaking. "He

attacked the reindeer-themed Christmas display down at the courthouse."

If he'd been at all tempted to even crack a smile, the slight wobble in her chin would have stopped him. As it was, he realized this was no laughing matter. And the wobble all but did him in.

"I don't think I can do this anymore," she breathed, and she looked as if her whole world had crumbled.

But for once in his life, Alec felt equipped to help. And what was more, he *wanted* to help. A desire to ease her burden had sparked to life somewhere deep inside him, and that wobble of her chin, coupled with her whisper of defeat, was like gasoline to the flame.

He'd witnessed her feisty streak, her spunky side and the dash of spoiled princess that she denied existed. And he'd seen her act more stubborn than any mule he'd come across. But seeing her vulnerable like this was something else entirely, probably because he knew how difficult it was for her to admit she didn't have everything under control.

He cupped her chin in his hand and tipped her face so she looked right up at him. "Everything is going to be okay," he said with the utmost authority.

"But..."

"Shh," he soothed and placed the tip of his finger against her lips. *So soft.* What was he doing? He'd promised himself he would keep his distance. Not that he'd done such a great job of keeping that promise thus far. "Wait here. Don't move."

When he returned with the dog, she was standing exactly where he'd left her. The fact that she'd obeyed him so precisely prompted his worry to spike. Zoey might be many things—half of them maddening—but *compliant* was nowhere on the list.

Once she set eyes on the dog, however, a flicker of life came back to her features. "Hold on a minute. What is that?"

"Well, she's not a reindeer, even though her name is Dasher." Despite himself, he grinned. Dasher. He'd suspected Zoey would love that. And Alec supposed he could live with it, even though it brought his life one step closer to a Hallmark Christmas special.

Her lips quirked into a reluctant smile. "Dasher. Cute."

Bingo.

The smile faded as quickly as it had come. But she no longer looked shattered. She looked ticked off, which was fine. Ticked off was better than devastated, in Alec's book. "What is she doing here?"

"I bought her. For you." He glanced down at Dasher sitting calmly at his feet and silently willed the dog to do something cute—trot over to Zoey, wag her tail. Anything.

"You bought me a dog?" The barest hint of a smile once again danced on her lips.

"Yes." He cleared his throat. He should explain. The dog wasn't a gift. Not exactly. But for some reason, he couldn't form the words.

She stared at Dasher and shook her head. "This is sweet, Alec, but I just can't..."

He held up his hands. "Wait. You don't understand."

"No, *you* don't understand." Her voice rose a hysterical octave. "I'm done. I can't handle the reindeer anymore. I've tried. I really have, but I just can't. And the very last thing I need right now is yet another animal."

"She's a reindeer-herding dog," he blurted. So much for finesse.

Her eyes widened. "What?"

Alec nudged Dasher with his foot, and she scooted toward Zoey. Finally. "She's a Finnish Lapphund. They're bred to keep an eye on reindeer. Brock Parker helped me find her. I thought she might be a solution to the ongoing Palmer problem."

A prolonged moment full of emotionally charged silence followed. The only sound Alec could hear, besides the gentle pant of Dasher's breath, was the beating of his own heart, which was undoubtedly pounding faster than normal.

Why was he so invested in her reaction? He normally didn't have this problem.

Granted, nothing about this situation was normal.

"You bought me a dog to babysit my troublesome reindeer?" she asked, her voice raw and shaky.

Alec took a step closer. He clenched his hands into fists to prevent himself from touching her again. "That's the idea."

Dasher nudged her way between them and pushed her furry head up and under Zoey's hand. Zoey's gaze fell on the dog. And then Alec's chest tightened as her eyes filled with tears.

"Please don't cry," he all but begged.

Alec had seen a lot in his life—things that haunted him, memories that had crawled under his skin and settled there for the long haul. But nothing had ever affected him quite like the sight of Zoey breaking down in soul-wrenching sobs.

"Please," he said again, his voice as raw as the ache in his chest.

Then, even though he knew better, he wrapped his arms around her and drew her in.

He tucked her head under his chin and held her tight as she wept. There was simply no stopping his arms from reaching for her. What was he supposed to do? Stand there and let her cry? Despite where he'd come from, he wasn't an unfeeling monster.

Far from it, apparently.

Holding Zoey, feeling her heart thundering against his, brought forth feelings in him that he'd never realized he was capable of. Her womanly scent—warm, sweet vanilla again—and the way she fit so perfectly in his embrace made him feel strong, manly, capable of taking care of her. Maybe even making her happy.

He struggled to swallow those misguided feelings. He'd bought her a dog, and she'd gotten a little emotional. That didn't mean he could allow himself to want things he had no business wanting.

But still he held her.

"Don't cry," he whispered against her hair. It tickled his nose and flooded his senses with that honeyed fragrance that made it hard for him to concentrate. "It's just a dog. Now everything's going to be fine."

"No." She shook her head against his chest. "It's not that."

He cupped her chin and searched her gaze. Her green eyes were brighter than ever before—as green as shamrocks. If only she hadn't been so vulnerable in that moment, if only she hadn't been crying, Alec might have kissed her right then and there. If only… "What is it?"

"It's too late." She swallowed. Alec traced the movement up and down her slender throat. "I've done something."

A thread of unease wound its way through him, but it was easy enough to ignore so long as Zoey was still in his embrace. He pressed an innocent kiss to the top of her head, telling himself it didn't really count. He still hadn't broken his promise to himself to stay away from her. He was fully capable of walking away and forgetting this whole episode. Probably.

"I told you everything is going to be fine," he whispered, and from somewhere deep inside—a place he'd tucked away and nearly forgotten, like an old faded photograph—the words of a Bible verse came to him. *And we know that in all things God works for the good of those who love him, who have been called according to his purpose.* Everything *would* be fine. How could it be too late? "What could you have possibly done?"

She pulled away from him. Her eyes had gone jade now, darkened with regret as she delivered the blow. "I've sold the reindeer."

Zoey held her breath and braced herself for Alec's reaction.

He flinched as though she'd slapped him. "What?" he said, incredulous.

"I've sold the reindeer." She sniffed and told herself she had no reason to feel guilty. The reindeer were her problem, not his. She was the one drowning in debt. She was the one struggling to find a way to keep everything together. Not Alec.

How was she supposed to know he would do something so…so nice? She glanced down at Dasher. Who'd ever heard of a reindeer-herding dog, anyway?

She closed her eyes. She knew good and well that this went beyond nice. Alec had thrown her a lifeline at a time when she needed it most. He'd really come through for her, but she hadn't even given him a chance.

"Oh." He sank into one of the kitchen chairs. He looked confused, as if trying to absorb what she'd told him. It was a difficult thing to watch. Far more difficult than Zoey had imagined it would be.

She cleared her throat. "I really had no choice."

It sounded like a weak excuse.

Maybe it was. But an hour ago, a minute ago, she'd believed it with every fiber of her being. How could she have thought otherwise as the Alaska State Trooper wrote out citation after citation and handed them to her with a grim smile?

He'd gone easy on her. He'd charged her with the bare minimum of offenses, but next time would be different. He'd promised her as much. She couldn't even conceive of a next time. The *bare minimum* fines had totaled almost three thousand dollars. It was as if she were dealing in Monopoly money now. A thousand here, a thousand there.

But there was no "pass go and collect two hundred dollars." There was only a constant outflow of money she didn't even have.

She was finished. She was so far in the red, she no longer knew what black looked like. If she didn't sell the reindeer, there would be no airplane in her future. Not now, anyway. And at the rate things were going, not ever.

She'd prayed and prayed for an answer. Maybe selling the reindeer was it.

Somehow that didn't seem right anymore.

"You've sold them. To whom?" Alec's expression turned stony. Obviously, the news had begun to sink in.

"To the only place that's made an offer," she answered cryptically.

He narrowed his gaze at her.

Was he really going to make her say it? Just thinking about it made her sick to her stomach. "I called the lawyer and told him to accept the offer from the commercial reindeer operation."

Alec dropped his head in his hands.

Zoey wanted to go to him. She wanted to comfort him—wrap him in a hug as he'd done for her when she'd been overcome with emotion or even just rest her hand on his shoulder. Anything.

But she knew she couldn't. She had no right.

She'd hurt him. Every bit as much as she'd hurt the reindeer.

"I'm sorry," she said.

He looked up, his face impassive. Emotionless.

A wave of sadness washed over her. She would have felt better if he'd said something mean, given her a cutting look or even yelled at her. Those things she could have handled.

But this cold indifference felt far worse. Only seconds ago, she'd been in his arms, and now everything had changed.

"It's fine," he said, meeting her gaze head-on. She searched his blue eyes for a hint that what had happened between them had been real—that she hadn't only imagined how right it had felt to be in his arms. But if he thought anything of the sort, he hid it well. "I'll start looking for a new job right away."

"There's no rush," she said a little too quickly. She didn't want to think about how lonely the ranch would seem without the reindeer. Without Alec. "You can stay in the guesthouse as long as you like."

"I'll keep that in mind," he muttered as he stood and crossed to the door.

The ache that had formed in Zoey's chest when she'd made the call to the lawyer's office burrowed deeper as Dasher scrambled to her feet and started to follow Alec.

The dog. What was she supposed to do with the dog now? "Um, what about the dog?"

"Keep her. She's yours." Alec opened the door. His wide shoulders filled the frame, but beyond him Zoey could see reindeer tossing their antlers and prancing through a snowfall so light and delicate it looked like rose petals falling to the ground.

In just a few days those reindeer would be gone.

A muscle flexed in Alec's back. Zoey could see it clear through the sleek black leather of his jacket and had a good idea just what that tension meant. Could he see it, too? The wistful, almost melancholy beauty of the scene playing out before them?

Of course he could. He'd have to be blind not to.

Alec fixed his gaze on the horizon, and without so much as a backward glance he stepped into the cold. Before the door clicked shut behind him, a gust of frosty air blew into the kitchen, ruffling the fur on Dasher's back and sending a shiver through Zoey that she felt deep in the marrow of her bones.

What have I done, Lord? She ran her fingertips over the dog's soft ears, and the cold settled into her so thoroughly that she wondered if she'd ever feel warm again. *What have I done?*

Chapter Ten

"You've done nothing wrong." Anya was adamant, shaking the money from one of the donation jars with more force than was necessary, perhaps to emphasize her point. "You can't beat yourself up about this."

Zoey watched dollar bills and a few coins spill out onto her kitchen table.

I should give this money back, she thought, guilt pooling in her stomach. *I failed. It's blood money now.*

"Seventy-eight dollars," Anya announced. "And five cents. And that's just the first jar."

Zoey eyed the stack of bills. "You're not suggesting I keep it."

"Why wouldn't you? People donated this money out of a desire to help."

"A desire to help *the reindeer.* Not me." She shook her head. "Whoever this money belongs to thought I was saving the reindeer. I'm not. I didn't. I'm a failure."

Anya quirked an eyebrow. "Could you get any more dramatic about it?"

"I'm worse than a failure." A wave of nausea—definitely not the first since breakfast—rolled over Zoey. "I'm a killer… a reindeer murderer."

"Wow. Yes, apparently you can get more dramatic about it. I severely underestimated your capacity for self-loathing."

"It's true. You know that old Rudolph movie from the sixties?"

Anya frowned, obviously wondering where the conversation was headed. "The one where Rudolph tries to cover his shiny red nose with mud?"

"Yes." Zoey had seen it dozens of times since she was a kid. Hadn't everyone? "Remember when all the other reindeer laughed at Rudolph and called him names? They seemed so heartless and cruel. Well, I'm worse than those mean reindeer."

"I'm beginning to get seriously worried about you, hon. Those reindeer aren't real. *It's a television show.* A pretty outdated one at that."

"It's a classic."

Anya shrugged. "Point taken. Sort of."

"I can't accept that money." Zoey dropped her head in her hands. "I won't."

"Okay, okay. I'll just put it in here while we add up the rest." Anya dropped the cash in a gallon-sized ziplock bag. Even if they filled the rest of that bag to the brim with twenty-dollar bills, it still wouldn't be enough money to get Zoey out of the trouble she was in.

If she kept it, which she most definitely was *not.*

Anya peered into another of the jars. "There's a fifty in this one."

Zoey glanced up, locking gazes with a pair of plastic googly eyes. "No, there's not."

"I'm afraid so." She slid the jar to the edge of the table. "Listen, something tells me we need to take a time-out."

A time-out sounded delicious. Like one of Gus's spectacular frosted chocolate-malt sundaes. Only better.

"You did the best you could, Zoey." Anya leaned forward

and took on a serious tone that Zoey had heard from her only a few times before, namely when they'd worked together at the coffee bar and something had gone wrong. "You don't know the first thing about reindeer. Most people in your position would have sold them in the very beginning, certainly after the fiasco at the airport."

Zoey nodded mutely.

"When does the sale become final?"

"Tomorrow morning." If everything went as planned, Zoey would leave the lawyer's office with check in hand and have just enough time to deposit it before heading to the airport to deliver her down payment and collect the keys to the Super Cub.

Do not pass go, do not collect two hundred dollars.

"What would happen if you changed your mind? If you didn't go through with it?"

"I wouldn't be able to buy the plane. The owner would start advertising it for sale again, and someone else would probably step up to the plate." She'd already begged the seller, a retired commercial pilot who'd bought a charter boat and relocated to the seaside town of Homer, Alaska, for more time. He'd refused. *Boats don't come cheap,* he'd said by way of explanation.

Neither did airplanes.

Anya pressed on. "Is there any chance the money in the rest of these jars could be enough to make up the difference and allow you to keep the reindeer?"

"No." It just wasn't possible. "Unless someone's written a four-figure check I'm unaware of."

Anya winced. "I doubt it."

"Then no."

"Good. You can stop feeling so guilty now, knowing you didn't have a choice." Anya nodded resolutely, but even so, her gaze drifted to the window and its view of the reindeer.

The herd was serene this morning. Quiet. No mad dashing about from one end of the fence to the other, no littering the white landscape with hay. If Zoey didn't know better, she'd think that somehow they knew what she'd done and were staging a silent protest.

Her throat grew tight. "I feel like I've failed him."

"Gus?"

"Yes," she choked out. Gus…the reindeer…even Alec.

She squeezed her eyes closed at the thought of Alec. She knew it was ridiculous to feel as though she'd let him down on some fundamental level. They weren't his reindeer, his burden. They were hers. And he might have been the one who found Gus, but he hadn't really known him. He'd never played Scrabble with Gus or gone out for ice cream with him.

None of that mattered, because when she closed her eyes all she could see was the look on Alec's face when she'd told him she'd sold the reindeer. He'd been so disappointed in her. He'd never said as much, of course.

He didn't have to.

"Um, Zoey?"

She opened her eyes and found Anya still gazing out the window, looking confused this time rather than nostalgic. "Yes?"

"There's a fox in the hen house," she said. "I mean, there's a bear on your reindeer farm. A baby bear. In the dead of winter. How is that possible?"

Zoey followed her gaze. "That's not a bear. That's Dasher, my dog." The dog did kind of look like a bear. She hadn't really noticed before.

Dasher was hunkered down in the snow beside Palmer. She'd curled herself into a ball beside the reindeer the moment he'd lain down, and except for resting her chin across the thick ridge of Palmer's neck, she hadn't moved since.

Anya frowned. "You have a dog now? A dog with a reindeer name?"

"Yes." Zoey sighed. "And yes. She was a gift from Alec."

"Alec gave you a dog? That's so sweet." She paused to mull it over. "And oddly personal for a Christmas gift, don't you think?"

"She wasn't a Christmas gift." Zoey didn't even want to think about Christmas. Could she just pretend it wasn't coming in fourteen days? Who killed off Rudolph two weeks before Christmas? "She's a reindeer-herding dog. He brought her here to help with Palmer."

"That's beyond sweet." Anya grinned. "That's really thoughtful. And sorta brilliant. Wow, look at her. She seems to have quite the work ethic."

Palmer rose to his feet, as did Dasher. When the reindeer took a step, so did the dog. It was uncanny. And pretty cute, too.

"She and Palmer are already as thick as thieves," Zoey said. "You really didn't know about it? Alec told me Brock helped him find her. Brock never mentioned it to you?"

That seemed strange. Brock and Anya shared everything. They even worked together.

"No." Anya shrugged. "Maybe Alec wanted to keep it a secret so he could surprise you."

"I guess so." A lump lodged in Zoey's throat. For some reason, the thought of Alec wanting to surprise her made her feel even worse.

"It really is a thoughtful gesture. You know, Zoey, it sounds like Alec might be growing rather fond of you."

Zoey's heart gave a wistful tug as she remembered Alec scooping her into his arms, the way he'd kissed the top of her head and tangled his fingertips in her hair. And most of all, the feeling of relief that had wanted to surge through her when he'd cradled her face in his hands and said with supreme confidence, *everything is going to be okay.*

For a sweet, sublime sliver of a moment, she'd finally known what it felt like to be able to depend on someone, to not have to go it alone. And in that instant, she could almost imagine what it felt like to be loved.

Almost.

And then she'd told him, *I've done something.*

No sooner had the words left her mouth than that heady feeling, that glittery rush of affection, had faded away like church bells on a cold winter's night. She'd felt it in the stiffening of his arms as he held her, and she could see it in the crippling sadness in his blue eyes.

It had been painful at the time. Somehow it seemed even more painful upon reflection.

"Alec…developing an affection for me? I don't think so," she said.

Not anymore.

Alec stood in the doorway of his little cabin, sipping coffee and watching Dasher's relentless pursuit of Palmer. The dog was remarkable. She seemed to have a good handle on the fact that Palmer, in particular, was her responsibility.

Alec had introduced the two of them late the night before, while he was still reeling from Zoey's news. He'd been so shell-shocked that he couldn't remember a single command from the long list the breeder had taught him when he and Brock had picked up the dog in Knik. He'd simply led Dasher to the far corner of the pasture where Palmer had been pouting all evening and said two words. *Watch him.*

Fifteen hours later, Dasher was still watching him.

Alec had to wonder if this crazy idea could have actually worked. If he'd gotten home a little sooner—an hour, two maybe—could he have convinced Zoey to hold out for one more day? And would Dasher have put an end to Palmer's escapades?

Not that such speculation mattered. It was too late.

It's too late. I've done something.

Zoey's pained confession came back to him again and again.

He wanted to be angry with her. He wanted it with every fiber of his being. She'd sold the reindeer without even consulting him first. He could have helped her. He *would* have helped her. He would have done whatever it took to save those beautiful animals, even Palmer. Especially Palmer. Didn't she know that?

He took a gulp of his coffee. No Northern Lights Inn gourmet Christmas blend this morning. He'd brewed it on the hot plate in his cabin, and it burned his throat as it went down. It was black and bitter, perfectly suited to his mood.

But as much as he wanted to blame Zoey, to rebuke her for what she'd done, he couldn't.

The farm wasn't his. He had no official place here. He didn't belong in Aurora any more than he belonged anywhere else.

The trouble was that he'd begun to feel at home on the Up on the Rooftop Reindeer Farm. Just thinking about that name made him roll his eyes, but as corny as it sounded, he'd come to look forward to waking up and spending his morning trudging through the snow with thirty-plus reindeer on his heels. He'd found something here that he didn't even realize he'd been looking for—peace. He was at peace here. He'd been so busy looking over his shoulder for most of his life that at first he hadn't recognized that feeling of serenity when he'd stumbled onto it.

But he recognized it now. Now that it was too late.

He didn't even want to think about what part Zoey played

in those warm, fuzzy feelings that had begun to assault him. But deep down he feared it was a big one.

He slung back the dregs of his coffee and let his gaze travel over the reindeer one last time. They were eerily still this morning. Most stood huddled against the wind. A few pawed elegant legs at the frosty ground, searching for lichen, a treasure they occasionally found buried beneath the snow.

Then there was Palmer.

It looked as though he'd decided to test the limits of Dasher's patience. The reindeer had begun to take sweeping side steps in an attempt to slip past the dog. But he was no match for Dasher. She dropped her head and fixed Palmer with a steely gaze that made the hair on the back of Alec's neck stand on end, even from thirty feet away. Undeterred, Palmer let out a snort. Dasher answered with an earsplitting bark. More shuffling ensued, and both of them were soon caught in a flurry of kicked-up snow. They almost appeared to be engaged in some sort of elaborate snow dance. Alec half expected the sky to break open in a blizzard.

He'd miss them. He'd miss Palmer, Dasher and all the rest of them. And he'd never ever eat a reindeer hotdog as long as he lived.

What about Zoey? Will you miss her, too?

Thinking about her living out here on her own made his insides hurt. It was a physical pain, like something mean and ugly trying to claw its way out.

He pushed it down, tamed it. Years of practice had made Alec adept at ignoring pain—emotional, physical, spiritual. It was a special talent he'd honed to perfection.

He pushed himself off the doorjamb and went inside. Standing around mooning over Zoey's decision wasn't his style. He had better things to do, like looking for a new job.

He opened his laptop and went on Craigslist. At the very

top of the page, an opening in Denali National Park caught his eye.

Wildlife Manager wanted. Start date: January 1.

He scanned the posting. The work was similar to what he'd done in the forest. And the pay was good. More than good, actually. It was double what Gus Henderson had promised to pay him for working at the reindeer farm. Located deep in the interior of Alaska, Denali was populated with an abundance of wildlife—grizzlies, wolves, moose, Dall sheep. Even reindeer. Best of all, it comprised over six million acres.

Which made it the perfect place to lose himself.

Again.

The barking would have awakened Zoey, if she'd been able to sleep. As it happened, she was still wide-awake when the yapping started.

She sat bolt upright in bed, heart hammering, until she remembered that, yes, she did indeed have a dog now. She collapsed back onto her pillow and prayed Dasher would stop. The temperature outside had dipped below fifteen degrees earlier in the night. Just the thought of dragging herself out of her warm bed to go outside and check on Dasher made her shiver.

She knew she should have let the dog sleep inside. She'd fully intended to do just that, even going so far as to make a little nest of blankets for Dasher at the foot of her bed. But Alec had reminded her that the whole point of the dog was to keep Palmer from escaping. How could Dasher keep an eye on Palmer if she was holed up in Zoey's bedroom?

"But won't she be cold?" Zoey had asked. "It's freezing outside. Literally."

"Have you seen the coat on that dog? She was bred for this. Trust me." Alec had looked exasperated. He'd looked like that a lot since she'd told him about selling the reindeer.

Not that she could blame him. She was exasperated with herself, too. The whole situation was exasperating.

"I'll make her a nice bed of straw, right beside Palmer. I can even cover her with a blanket. Will that make you feel better?" he'd asked.

"I guess." She'd finally relented and pledged right then and there to buy the poor dog a down coat from the pet store. Or at the very least, a sweater.

Not that any of that would matter after tonight. The reindeer were due to be hauled off shortly after the papers were signed. In all likelihood they would be gone by the time she returned from closing the deal on her airplane. Dasher would sleep at the foot of Zoey's bed after that, if the dog still wanted to have anything to do with her. Zoey had her doubts. Why would a reindeer-herding dog want to hang out with someone who'd sent so many reindeer off to their doom?

God, please help me make sense of all this.

Zoey lay very still in the darkness, and the barking stopped.

Why did Gus leave me all these reindeer? And why did things have to go so horribly wrong?

She blinked back a fresh wave of tears.

Just, why?

An answer wasn't immediately forthcoming, and even if it were, Zoey would never have heard it over the new barking fit erupting from the backyard. This time the yaps sounded frantic, almost urgent.

A chill of alarm ran up Zoey's spine.

She tossed off the covers and slipped into her parka without even bothering to change out of her pajamas. By the time she found her mittens, jammed her feet into snow boots and ran outside, Alec was already running from the guest cabin toward the pasture.

She'd never been so happy to see him before, not even

when she'd mistakenly thought she could single-handedly force Palmer off the airport runway. Once she'd hopped out of bed, a whole host of terrifying possibilities had entered her head. What if Dasher was trying to tell her that the reindeer were in danger? Would she run outside and find herself eye to eye with a rogue moose? Or worse, a wolf? This was Alaska, after all.

She ran as fast as she could toward Alec, her feet catching a few times in ruts and holes the reindeer had dug in the snow. It was late. Zoey wasn't sure what time exactly, but the night was already inky black and the moon hovered high in the sky, a tiny sliver that bathed the pasture in only the faintest beam of light. Dasher was still carrying on as if the world were coming to an end, her barks now punctuated with mournful wails.

Zoey threw herself at Alec once she reached him, clutching his arms, afraid to look beyond his powerful, reassuring frame. "What's happening?"

He held her by the shoulders and planted her firmly in place. "Stay right here."

She nodded mutely, feeling absolutely ridiculous while he turned to investigate.

This was silly. She was a grown woman.

She peered around Alec. "What's happening?"

He said nothing, and she couldn't see a thing. So she squared her shoulders, pretended she wasn't afraid and marched forward until she stood beside him.

There was no wolf, no moose. No abominable snowman. Just Dasher standing toe-to-toe with Palmer as the reindeer paced in front of the fence.

"What's all the fuss about?" Zoey asked.

Alec stared down at her. "I thought I told you to stay behind me. Do you ever do as you're told?"

"No." She crossed her arms and tried unsuccessfully to

suppress a shiver. It was freezing out here. Poor Dasher was probably just staging a protest against being left outside. "But be honest. Would you really like me more if I did?"

He cracked the slightest of smiles. "Probably not."

Dasher let out another earsplitting bark.

Zoey threw up her hands. "Seriously, what is her problem?"

"Maybe she knows something we don't." Alec aimed his steely glare at Palmer. "I think our friend here might be trying to make a break for it."

"You checked the fence, right?"

He nodded. "Yep. No holes, no gaps, no breakage of any kind."

Zoey opened her mouth to say something else, but before she could utter a word, Palmer did something that put an abrupt end to all the speculation. He gathered his feet under him, and in a single powerful, elegant move he leaped straight in the air. He soared easily up and over Dasher and then right over the fence. He landed on the other side with only the barest of thuds then trotted off into the darkness.

Zoey and Alec looked at one another and then back at Palmer's quickly disappearing backside.

Dasher barked again, as if trying to remind them that she was still there. Ready and willing to get to work.

"Come on, girl." Alec jogged toward the gate, unlatched it and swung it open. "Go get him."

Dasher lived up to her name and took off after the reindeer, leaving nothing but a cloud of snow and straw behind her.

Zoey blinked after her, still trying to process everything she'd just witnessed. "Will she really bring him back?"

"She should. Let's at least give her a chance." Alec grinned at Zoey. "Mystery solved, I guess. Now we know how Palmer's been escaping."

"I had no idea. Can they all do that?"

"Haven't you heard? Reindeer can fly." He eyed the legs of her pajama bottoms poking out from beneath her parka. Red flannel, decorated with moose that had Christmas lights tangled in their antlers. They were her favorite Christmas pair. "I would think you of all people would know that."

She pulled her parka a bit tighter. "I'm being serious. Can they all leap like that?"

"Sure, they can jump. Pretty high when they want to, apparently."

Jumping wouldn't have accurately described what she'd seen. Neither did *leaping,* really. Alec's mocking aside, what Palmer had done seemed more like flying than anything. As she'd watched him, it *felt* like flying. The look on his face as he'd soared high over the fence had captured everything that swelled inside Zoey when she was in the cockpit, as if he'd experienced the same awe-inspiring joy she always did at that perfect moment when the wheels of the airplane left the ground.

She'd talked about that joy before with other pilots, and even they didn't fully grasp it. Except Gus.

Gus.

Zoey's heart lurched.

And suddenly everything that had transpired since Gus's sudden death came together in perfect, poetic clarity. It all made sense—Gus, the reindeer, even the name he'd given the farm. Up on the Rooftop. How had she not seen it before?

"That's why Gus had them." A sense of wonder welled up inside her, and she half expected her own feet to lift off the ground. "They can fly."

Alec leveled her with a sardonic look. "No, they can't. I wasn't being literal, sweetheart."

There it was again. *Sweetheart.*

One of these days, he's going to call me that and he's going to actually mean it.

She blinked. Clearly, she was dreaming. Or sleep deprived. Because Alec was the last thing she needed to worry about now.

She shook her head in an effort to clear her thoughts. "That wasn't any ordinary jump. That was the closest thing to flying I've ever seen from any kind of deer. Admit it—that was something special."

Again, the corner of his mouth lifted into a reluctant grin. "I have to admit it was impressive."

"Don't you see? That's why Gus had the reindeer. Flying was everything to him. The reindeer were a living embodiment of his love of flight. And that's why he left them to me." She swallowed around the rapidly forming lump in her throat. "Because he knew I was the only one who would understand."

Finally.

God had answered her prayers. In the most spectacular way possible, He'd shown her why Gus had kept the reindeer and why he'd wanted her to have them after he was gone. She had her answers.

Then why did she feel so heartsick?

"Here they come," Alec whispered as Palmer trotted toward the gate, Dasher nipping at his heels, driving him home with relentless determination.

Zoey wiped a tear from her cheek with one of her mittens as Alec clicked the gate closed behind them. "That dog is really something."

"She is, isn't she?" Alec walked back toward her, a hint of sadness in his features.

She knew they were both thinking the same thing—it would have worked. Dasher could have kept Palmer in line.

If only there'd been more time.

Defeated, at least for the time being, Palmer settled himself near the barn. He lowered onto his knees then rolled onto his side. Within seconds, he was snoring loud enough to prompt an avalanche. Dasher shook a layer of snow off her coat before stretching out against Palmer's side and resting her chin across the reindeer's belly.

"Look at them." Zoey bit her lip to keep the tears at bay. "They're so cute together."

Alec nodded, and his gaze dropped to his feet. "It will be a shame to split them up. They seem to get on really well."

"They do. It's funny. A dog and a reindeer. They're so different from each other. Who would have known?"

He lifted his head, and his blue eyes fixed on hers. "I guess it's true what they say. Sometimes opposites attract."

That floaty feeling returned, and she felt as if she might lift right off the ground like Palmer and drift up into the starry Alaskan sky. "I guess so."

He took a step closer. The air between them grew still and warm. As warm as a summer day. "Zoey?"

He said her name as if it was a question. She could hear a world of emotion in his voice—pain, sorrow, regret. But in the midst of all that, hope rose to the top. And right then, with the moonlight casting purple shadows on the snowy pasture and starlight shimmering overhead, Zoey wanted the answer to that question to be yes.

His gaze dropped to her mouth.

Yes.

He slipped off one of his gloves and reached out to touch her face. His fingertip left a trail of shivers in its wake, and she had to stop herself from reaching up on tiptoe and pressing her lips against his.

Yes, her heart cried.

But she couldn't. If she kissed him now, she'd never be able to watch him go. And once the reindeer were gone, Alec wouldn't be far behind.

First her parents, then Gus. Now Alec. She knew it wasn't exactly a fair comparison. Her parents and Gus had died, and Alec was still very much alive. But it didn't feel altogether different. It felt more similar than she cared to admit. Maybe because the end result was the same. It seemed this was always happening—people she cared about disappearing, leaving her alone.

She'd grown accustomed to it. She could handle it.

So long as she didn't kiss him.

She took a step backward, out of his reach. "I should go back to bed."

His jaw clenched, and his blue eyes gave away his hurt. Hurt, but not surprise. "You're right. It's late."

Too late.

"Good night, Alec." It took every ounce of self-control she possessed to turn and walk away from him.

"Good night," he whispered behind her, his warm breath dancing a sad waltz on the back of her neck.

And it sounded more like goodbye.

Chapter Eleven

Alec's motorcycle was long gone by the time Zoey left for the lawyer's office the next morning to sell the reindeer. She wondered where he'd gone then reminded herself that she shouldn't care. The reindeer had been fed, and their trough was filled with fresh water that hadn't yet begun to freeze around the edges. Dasher was sprawled on her belly on a fresh pile of straw, chewing on a giant rawhide bone while keeping one eye stubbornly trained on Palmer at all times.

Everything was in order. So she really shouldn't care where Alec had gotten himself off to.

But much as she hated to admit it, she did care. Very much.

Alec was different. There was just something about him that made her want to break down the walls she'd so carefully constructed around her heart. She'd had no trouble keeping her past boyfriends at arm's length, but a single look from Alec's cool gray eyes was enough to make those walls feel less like a safety measure and more like a prison of her own making. Cracks were beginning to form in her resistance. Cracks that both terrified and thrilled Zoey.

She should have let him kiss her the night before. Better yet, she should have kissed him herself. Life was short.

How many of her loved ones had to die in order for her to learn that lesson?

She'd paused to watch the reindeer for a few minutes before climbing into her car, thinking that right now they were the best example of the fleeting nature of life. How much time would they have, once the new owner took them away this afternoon? She'd wanted to cry just thinking about it. So she'd whispered goodbye, blown a kiss at Palmer and left. She hoped they would be gone by the time she came home from closing on the airplane. She didn't think she could watch them being hauled off.

The drive to the lawyer's office was agonizingly slow. Zoey was caught behind a snowplow for a good part of the way, which gave her time to see three planes take off from the runway behind the Northern Lights Inn. One of them was a Super Cub like hers, only red instead of yellow. As she watched it climb above the hotel, its wings going wobbly for a second before steadying out, she waited for the familiar lump to spring to her throat—the one she always got when she witnessed a takeoff.

It never came.

Odd.

She fixed her gaze on the back bumper of the snowplow in front of her and, for once, willed herself to think about something other than flying. She was just spooked, that was all. Once the paper work was in order and she had a big check in hand, things would be different. She would have her airplane. Finally, she'd be able to call herself a real charter pilot.

How long had she waited for this? Years.

Years of pinching every penny. Years of ramen noodles for dinner. Years of shopping for clothes at the church thrift shop.

Years.

And she'd known those silly reindeer for all of a week.

Life is short, she reminded herself. *You need to seize the moment when you can. Opportunities like this don't come along every day. You've worked long and hard to make this happen. You can't let a bunch of reindeer come between you and your dreams.*

Nevertheless, the pep talk felt hollow as she guided the car into the parking lot of the lawyer's office and shifted into Park. She gripped the steering wheel and bowed her head.

God, please. I'm doing the right thing, aren't I?

But when she closed her eyes, all she could see was Palmer…soaring high in the sky, like something out of a Christmas fairy tale.

Palmer.

And Alec, his handsome face lit with an astonished smile. She'd never seen him smile like that before. The rarity of the expression made it all the more memorable.

Alec, the Scrooge—Alec, who'd never in his life had a Christmas tree—had smiled like a giddy little kid when Palmer soared up into the sky.

Together, they'd witnessed something special the night before. Something spectacular. And thanks to her, something that would never happen again.

Zoey's heart stuttered. She opened her eyes and realized her hands were shaking. She reached for the seat belt and couldn't even get it unclicked.

What are you doing? Get out of the car. Your future is right through those doors.

After somehow managing to spring herself free from the seat belt, she practically ran the short distance to the lawyer's office. Not an easy task in four inches of slush, but possible. Very possible. The hem of her jeans might be soaked through, but by the end of the day, she'd be the person with soaked jeans *and* an airplane. For once in her life, she would be a strong, independent businesswoman instead of the town orphan.

The receptionist gave a little start when Zoey burst through the door. "Miss Hathaway, you're here. Great! Everyone is expecting you. They're all waiting in the conference room. Can I get you anything? Water? Coffee?"

"No, thank you. I'm fine." Was she fine? Was she really?

She concentrated on putting one foot in front of the other as she entered the conference room and made her way to the empty chair beside her lawyer's seat.

"Good morning, Zoey," he said. His name was David. David Farmer. And he had a kind face, which made her feel better to a minuscule degree.

"Morning." She sat down.

The two men seated on the opposite side of the table smiled and introduced themselves as the president and the CEO of the Bowmaker Commercial Food Group.

Zoey gulped. Food Group? That didn't sound good. Not good at all. She tried not to think too much about it while David read over the particulars of the agreement. Instead, she concentrated on the wording of the contract. But after a minute or two of *wherebys* and *heretofores,* her mind began to wander. David's voice drifted further and further away until it became little more than background noise. Soon all she could hear were the soft footfalls of reindeer paws in the snow, their hooves clicking with each step.

She shook her head. Now she was hearing things? Perfect.

She refocused on the present and realized the clicking noise she'd heard wasn't a reindeer at all. Rather, it was David absently clicking the button of the retractable pen in his hand. She wondered if, from now on, every time she heard the click of a pen she'd have visions of reindeer.

She wished Alec had never told her about the special tendons that reindeer had in their back hooves. She wished she didn't know how velvety soft their noses felt against the palm of her hand when she offered them treats. She wished reindeer were like zebras or lions, and no one wanted to eat them.

She wished a lot of things.

"Do you have any questions?" David asked.

"Um, yes." She sat up straighter and smiled at the men seated across from her. "I was wondering if you might consider using part, or perhaps all, of my reindeer for your breeding program. Instead of…you know…" *Eating them.*

Had she just said *my* reindeer instead of Gus's reindeer?

The Bowmaker executives exchanged wary glances.

David gave her a tense smile. "Zoey, the agreement doesn't specify how the buyers will use the reindeer. Once they take possession of the livestock, it's really their call."

Livestock. The word seemed to lodge in her temple with a sharp pain. "I understand. But I was hoping you might consider sparing them from…from…"

"From slaughter?" the man who'd identified himself as the CEO asked, and Zoey decided she didn't like him much. "I'm sorry, but we can't make promises about the circumstances of any individual animals. We haven't even evaluated them yet."

"I see," she said.

There was a moment of silence, then all three men looked relieved that she'd stopped asking questions.

She wondered what the evaluation process was like. Did they measure the body fat of the reindeer? Why hadn't she put them all on diets once she'd decided to sell? Scrawny reindeer couldn't be too appetizing.

"But…" she started again. But what?

But my *reindeer are special.*

Since when had she started thinking of Gus's reindeer as hers? Technically, they *were* hers. But she'd always thought of them as Gus's.

Until now, apparently.

She took a deep breath. "Gentlemen, I understand where

you're coming from. I do. It's just that the reindeer, one in particular, are special."

The CEO furrowed his brow. "One in particular?"

"Yes. His name is Palmer. Perhaps we could come to some sort of understanding about him." She swallowed, feeling terrible about throwing the other thirty reindeer under the bus. Then panic swarmed in her belly when she realized they didn't have name tags. Or collars. How would the new owners know their names? Was it too late to make a list?

David turned toward her. "Isn't Palmer the one that's been causing you so much trouble?"

"Trouble?" the president and CEO asked in unison.

"Well, um, yes. But…"

"Weren't all the expenses you've incurred due to Palmer's behavior instrumental in your decision to sell the herd?" David asked.

Must he dwell on Palmer's mischievous streak? At the rate David was going, Palmer would be on Bowmaker's naughty list before they even set eyes on him.

"That's true," she admitted.

What was wrong with her? She was losing it. Yesterday she'd been so frustrated with Palmer that she'd agreed to sell off all the reindeer, and now here she was, begging for a pardon on his behalf.

"Miss Hathaway," the president said calmly, resting his palms on the table. "We understand this has been a difficult time for you. And we're sorry for your loss. From what we've heard, Gus Henderson was a remarkable man. The fact of the matter, though, is that he left you these reindeer but failed to make arrangements for their care. Selling them is a perfectly understandable option."

David cleared his throat. "Actually, Mr. Henderson was in the process of making arrangements for the care of the herd in the event of his death at the time of his heart attack."

"What?" Zoey's breath caught in her throat. This was certainly new information.

But did it change things?

"Yes." David nodded. "He'd begun the process of purchasing a life-insurance policy, with the idea that the proceeds could be used for the care and maintenance of the reindeer. Unfortunately, he passed away before the purchase was finalized."

Gus had wanted to buy a life-insurance policy so she could care for the reindeer?

For some reason, this made Zoey feel like crying. She sniffed. "Oh."

"Like I said, Gus Henderson was a fine man. But without that policy in place, young lady, you've got a challenging financial predicament on your hands. We can make that problem disappear. Perhaps this will make you feel better about your decision." The CEO slid a rectangular slip of paper across the table toward her.

It was a cashier's check, made payable to her. And it was for the largest chunk of money she'd ever gotten at one time. She blinked at it, all the while making mental calculations. With this kind of money, she could pay off the FAA fine and the citations Palmer had incurred, plus have the money she needed for her airplane. She could even pay Alec what she owed him.

Alec.

The thought of him prompted another moment of panic. Why did she feel as though she was letting him down every bit as much as the reindeer?

"Zoey, do you have any more questions?" David asked.

She let her gaze fall on the check again and its dollar amount. *All those zeros.* "No, I guess not."

Her mouth grew dry, and she suddenly had difficulty swallowing.

"Here you go, then." David smiled and offered her his pen.

Zoey stared at it.

Don't be stupid. Take the pen. Just reach out, take it and sign the papers.

Just as she began to reach for it, he pressed the button again.

Click.

Zoey blinked. Hard. She withdrew her hand.

"I'm sorry," she whispered.

The CEO leaned forward, frowning. "Sorry? I don't understand."

He wasn't the only one.

Zoey didn't understand what she was going to do for money or how she would ever be able to afford her airplane, but one thing was crystal clear—she couldn't sell those reindeer.

"I'm sorry," she repeated then slid the check back across the table. "I just can't do this."

The sun dipped below the mountains as Alec exited the highway and cruised back into Aurora. Even with his protective winter gear—chaps, gaiter and thick leather gloves—the cold was beginning to get to him. Probably because he'd ridden his bike over two hundred miles to Denali and back since sunup.

If he was going to stay in Alaska, it might be time to invest in some heated clothing. And it looked as if he was going to do just that. Stay. Although not in Aurora. Not even close. Alaska was a big state—the biggest.

The job at Denali National Park was his. The senior park ranger who'd interviewed him had already called his references back in Washington before he'd even arrived for the interview. He'd been impressed enough with what he'd heard that the interview itself had seemed more like a formality. The only blip on the radar had been when he'd asked Alec why he'd left the forest to work as a ranch hand on a reindeer farm.

He'd made some lame excuse, said he needed a change of scenery, which was technically true. He'd needed to go somewhere where his past wouldn't find him, and that had required a radical change of scenery. The senior park ranger didn't appear to have any qualms about the explanation. In fact, he'd been pleased that Alec had some experience with reindeer since caribou were plentiful at the park.

Alec wasn't sure quite how he felt about that. He'd been reluctant to work with reindeer in the first place, and now they'd managed to burrow their way under his skin. He dreaded returning to the farm and facing the empty pasture.

Deep down he felt guilty for not being there to deal with their transport. He should have been there when the truck came to pick them up. Didn't that fall under his job description?

He just couldn't do it. He couldn't watch them being taken away, knowing what was bound to happen to them and not able to do a thing to stop it.

Zoey could fire him if she so chose. She probably *should* fire him. He'd been paid to work through the end of December, but what was he supposed to do on the farm until then without the reindeer to care for—toss frost-covered Frisbees for Dasher all day?

No, thank you.

He gritted his teeth at the thought of leaving. He didn't know why. Taking the job in Denali made perfect sense. The money was good, and right now his bank balance could use a little boost. He'd spent a sizable chunk of change on Dasher.

I bought a fancy reindeer-herding dog for a woman who no longer owns any reindeer.

It would have been funny if it weren't so sad.

As he turned his bike off the main road and headed up

the drive toward the now-reindeerless reindeer farm, he did his best to shake his somber mood. Or at the very least, hide it. He had a feeling he was about to find Zoey in a puddle of tears. Though he suspected she thought otherwise, he doubted even the purchase of her airplane would fully make up for the loss of the reindeer. And even though every man, woman and child in Aurora would be happy to lend her a shoulder to cry on, Alec knew good and well she'd be holed up on the farm all alone. Zoey was the type of woman who would rather carry the reindeer away one by one on her back than have anyone pity her.

Somebody needed to be there to pick up the pieces. He figured he might as well be the one to do it. To comfort her. Why exactly he thought that duty should fall on his shoulders was a mystery he couldn't begin to fathom.

But when he pulled his motorcycle alongside Zoey's car, the pasture wasn't quite as barren as he'd expected. Reindeer dotted the landscape, poking at the snow with their noses and tossing hay into the air with their antlers as if today were any ordinary day.

So he hadn't missed them being hauled away, after all.

His chest tightened when he climbed off his bike and spotted Zoey leaning against the fence, wrapped in a thick fleece blanket. She was wearing that ratty plaid hat again—the one he suspected had belonged to Gus. A mug with a candy cane sticking out of it was clutched in one of her hands, and with the other she was petting Palmer. The reindeer stretched his neck across the fence, leaning into her touch with a look of sheer rapture on his face.

Oh, boy.

This cozy goodbye scene was a recipe for disaster if he'd ever seen one. What was she doing? Trying to torture herself?

He'd never been one for long, emotional goodbyes. Even when Camille had told him she no longer wanted to marry him, the matter had been handled like a business arrangement. There were things to be said for a clean break.

"Zoey," he ground out, walking toward her with purpose. There weren't going to be enough tissues in the world if he let her love on Palmer like that until they came to take him away.

She spun her head around. "Oh, hi, Alec. I'm glad you're home. I…"

"Stop." He held up his hands. "Just stop. Let's go inside."

"I don't want to go inside."

"Zoey, please listen. For once." He jerked his head toward the house.

She ignored him, of course. "I made some hot chocolate. Want some?"

He frowned at her mug, aiming most of his annoyance at the candy cane. "I'm not exactly the hot-chocolate type."

"Seriously? Who doesn't like hot chocolate?" Palmer craned his head toward the candy cane, as if he were trying to drive her point home. Zoey laughed. "Careful, Palmer. You'll end up on Santa's naughty list."

She was doing it again. Driving him crazy. He couldn't help but wonder if it was intentional. Or maybe she was just in massive denial.

He waved a hand between her and the reindeer. "Do you really think this is the best idea? Considering…" There was no pretty way to finish that thought, so he didn't. She had to know what he meant.

"Actually, there's something I need to tell you."

And that was when he noticed the dog was missing. The last time she'd had something to tell him, it was that she'd sold the reindeer. So the absence of the dog struck him as slightly ominous. "Wait a minute. Where's Dasher? Have you sent her packing, too?"

Zoey's emerald eyes flashed. "She's inside, curled up by

the fire. I thought she looked cold. And for your information, no one's leaving. Everyone is staying right here."

His head swam. And even as he stood there, trying to wrap his mind around what she was saying, snow from Denali National Park was still trapped in the treads of his hiking boots. A single thought throbbed in his consciousness. *Not everyone.*

He swallowed. "The sale didn't go through?"

She shook her head, and the anger in her pretty green eyes melted into tears. "I couldn't go through with it. When the time came to sign the papers, I literally couldn't even make myself pick up the pen."

"Wow. I don't even know what to say." A number of things sprang immediately to mind. Chief among them was a simple, sincere prayer. *Thank You, Lord.*

She grinned up at him through her tears. "Surprised?"

"Yes. Pleasantly so." He was forced to clear his throat.

To his horror, he realized he was getting choked up himself. Over a bunch of reindeer, no less.

"Good," Zoey whispered.

She set her mug down on the fence railing, and before Alec even realized what she was up to, she'd reached up on tiptoe and wrapped her arms around him, blanket and all.

He hadn't had time to properly prepare himself for her closeness. All at once he was enveloped in her warmth, in her softness. In her. His head spun, overwhelmed by a flurry of sensation. Zoey's usual vanilla scent, kissed by the faintest hint of candy cane. The sparkle of snowflakes that had gathered in her hair. And above all else, the undeniable feeling of completion that came over him when she stepped into his arms.

Holding her felt right.

It felt so right, it almost frightened the life out of him.

"Zoey." He dipped his head and murmured against her hair. "What does this mean, exactly?"

She tipped her head up to meet his gaze with a smile on her lips, but he could see the subtle melancholy behind it. "It means I've accepted the fact that Gus's reindeer are now mine. They were a part of him. A part of him I wouldn't want to let go, even if I could."

"And your airplane?" He had to ask, even though he feared he knew the answer already.

A tear slipped down her cheek. "There is no airplane. Not anymore. Maybe someday."

"Oh, sweetheart." He gathered her back into an embrace and held her tight.

He held her as she cried, both happy tears and tears of loss. He held her while the last lavender glow of twilight vanished into the indigo night.

He held her until a loud crunching noise dragged them back to reality.

Alec chuckled. "I think Palmer might have stolen your candy cane."

"Perfect," she said as she stepped out of his arms.

Then she bit her lip, drawing every bit of Alec's attention to her mouth. "It won't hurt him, will it?"

He paused for a beat, trying to remember what they'd been talking about.

Palmer. The candy cane.

Oh, yeah. "It was just a nibble. I think he'll be fine, although I wouldn't let him make a habit out of it."

She pulled the mug out of Palmer's reach. "You're like a walking encyclopedia when it comes to these guys. What would I do without you around here?"

What would I do without you around here?

He told himself it was just an expression. She didn't mean anything by it. She couldn't. She would be perfectly fine after he'd gone.

"There's something else we need to talk about," he said.

"Oh?" she asked, reaching out to pet Palmer with her free hand.

Palmer grunted with delight. Alec had never seen him so happy. It was as though he somehow knew he'd been granted a last-minute reprieve, like a prisoner on death row. And Zoey looked pretty happy herself now, especially considering she was a pilot without an airplane.

Too happy.

Tell her. Just do it. Tell her about the job in Denali. "It can wait. Come with me." He reached for her hand.

She gave him a quizzical look as she fell in step beside him. "Where are we going?"

There wasn't much Alec could do about how much she'd sacrificed to keep the reindeer. He couldn't buy her an airplane. But there was one thing…

He gave her hand a squeeze. "I'm taking you flying."

Zoey let Alec lead her to the driveway where, as she'd expected, there was no airplane waiting to whisk them away. "I'm confused. Am I supposed to flap my arms or something?"

He raised a sardonic brow. "Close your eyes, Miss Smarty Pants."

She wasn't sure what he was up to, but she obeyed. Why not? After the emotional day she'd had, she didn't have the energy to argue.

"Here. I don't want you to freeze to death," he murmured.

He lifted the blanket from her shoulders and slid her arms into a heavy leather jacket. Zoey's senses went on high alert.

It was his voice. Without the benefit of sight, his deep, masculine tone was impossible to ignore. It rumbled through her, from the soles of her feet to the tips of her fingers. She forgot to breathe for a minute, until she realized he'd tucked her into his own jacket. It still carried the warmth of his body. And his scent—a heady combination of fir trees and cold mountain air. She took a deep breath.

"You can open your eyes now," he rumbled again.

She let her lashes flutter open and found Alec sitting astride his motorcycle, smiling and thrusting a helmet toward her.

She hesitated. Hadn't she nearly fallen off the last time she'd gotten on this thing? "Wait. I'm not sure if this is such a good idea."

"It's the closest thing to an airplane I've got. Trust me. When we get out on the back roads and you stretch your arms out wide under the starry sky, you'll feel like you're flying." He winked, and a zing of electricity shot through her.

He made it sound awfully fun. And oddly romantic.

Although she probably wouldn't know how to respond to a romantic gesture on the rare occasion that one presented itself. She'd made a habit out of avoiding anything remotely resembling a romantic overture. She'd once feigned a stomach virus just to dodge an invitation to the church Valentine's Day dance.

Not that deep down she was pining for romance. She needed a boyfriend like she needed another three dozen reindeer. Romance was the last thing she should be thinking about. Her life was a mess right now. She had no job, no airplane and a rapidly dwindling supply of money. And she'd had about as much loss and heartache as she could take. She'd been on her own for a long time now. Life was comfortable this way. Safe. So long as her heart was her own, the rug couldn't be swept out from under her again. Eventually, love only led to one thing. Loss.

Alec's lips curved into a naughty grin. "You're not still scared of my motorcycle, are you?"

Now, how was she supposed to ignore that kind of accusation?

"For the record, I was never afraid of this thing." She gave her chin a defiant lift. "And I'm still not."

"Sure you're not." He winked again, and Zoey could practically see the sarcastic, unspoken *sweetheart* dancing in his eyes.

"You've managed to convince me." She took the helmet from him and slipped it into place. "Or coerce me. One of the two."

"You might want to try hanging on this time. At least until we get out on the open road. Just a suggestion," he said as he gave the chin strap of her helmet a gentle tug. His gaze fixed with hers, and he seemed almost reluctant to let go. But that didn't make sense. She was probably imagining things. Hadn't this ride been his idea in the first place?

She gulped. "Will do."

Then she climbed on behind him and wrapped her arms around his waist. She already felt impossibly small next to him, practically swimming in his heavy leather jacket and helmet. His sizable muscles beneath her hands made her feel even tinier. And ridiculously feminine. Warmth flooded her cheeks.

Alec cast a glance over his shoulder, and Zoey was thankful for the darkness. "Ready?"

"As ready as I'll ever be."

"Promise me you'll do your best to think of it as an airplane. Before long, you'll think you're flying."

Her heart turned a little somersault. Whether he intended it or not, this *was* romantic. And sweet. Really sweet.

The bike thundered to life beneath them, and she tightened her grip on Alec's waist. Then they were rolling slowly down the driveway. The hard-packed snow made the ride a little bumpy, and Zoey tried to think of it as turbulence. But when Alec turned onto the road, which had been freshly swept by the snowplow, everything smoothed out.

He accelerated, and Zoey closed her eyes. Adrenaline surged through her veins. A familiar feeling of joy swelled up inside her—the same thrilling sensation that always seized her on the moment of takeoff.

He's right. We're flying.

She lifted her face to the night sky. The cold wind nipped at her nose, and a gentle flurry of snowflakes swirled overhead. The engine roared even louder and they went faster. And faster. Until the stars glittering above looked as though they were falling and spinning all around them.

She wasn't sure how long they rode. And she didn't care. When they reached the outskirts of Aurora, Alec slowed the bike to a stop at a scenic overlook. The entire town spread before them, even the reindeer farm, barely visible at the foot of the mountains.

"Beautiful, isn't it?" Zoey whispered.

Alec turned and let his gaze travel over her face. Slowly. Deliberately. "Yes, beautiful."

Her throat grew dry. "Thank you for this…for taking me flying. It's just what I needed. How did you know?"

He shrugged one of his well-formed shoulders. "I suppose I've come to know a few things about you."

Do you know how badly I want you to kiss me right now?

Her heart pounded so hard she thought she might fall off the bike. A surge of anticipation uncoiled in her belly. Her head spun in a dizzying imitation of what it was like to defy gravity. She felt as though she could float up so high, she could scrape the bottom of the clouds with the tips of her fingers. "Is that so?"

She leaned a fraction closer. Alec drew in a sharp, shaky inhale.

Oh, he knows.

She laid a hand on his firm chest, and in the brief moment before he gathered her hand in his and removed it, she felt the telltale thump of his heart that told her he wanted that kiss just as badly as she did.

"Zoey." Her name was a ragged whisper on his lips. "There's something I need to tell you."

He reached for her other hand. With both her hands nestled in his, he stared down at their interlocked fingers for a long, silent moment. Then he looked back up at her, and something in his blue eyes caused her breath to catch in her throat. Right then she knew that whatever he needed to tell her wasn't good news.

She cleared her throat. Whatever it was, she could take it. Hadn't she been on the receiving end of bad news enough to become an expert at hearing it?

"What is it?" she asked flatly.

"I've found another job. At Denali National Park. I start the first of the year." He said it quickly.

So quickly that, for a moment, she thought she'd misheard him. How could he have found another job so soon? "Already?"

He nodded. "Yes. It's a great position, actually. The money is good, and there are even reindeer at the park."

"Well, that's..." *Devastating.* She pasted on a smile. "Wonderful. I'm so happy for you."

"I'm sorry if this leaves you in a bind. If I'd known you were keeping the reindeer..."

What? You would have stayed?

Not likely.

Alec wasn't the type. Even with her limited experience with men, Zoey could tell that much about him. The fact that all of his worldly possessions fit in a single duffel bag had to mean something, didn't it?

"Don't be silly. I can handle things on my own just fine." Her words came out more harshly than she'd intended.

Alec narrowed his eyes at her. “Of course you can. What was I thinking?”

“That I’d be upset? That I needed you?” She let out a laugh that bordered on hysterical. “Well, I don’t.”

“Clearly.” He turned back around and cranked the motorcycle back to life.

The ride home was faster, like a jet riding on a tail wind. Zoey half expected the wheels to float clear off the pavement. In a moment of bravery—or insanity—she lifted her arms from Alec’s waist and held them up in the air like the wings of a plane.

She was flying again.

The arctic wind bit at her face, stung her eyes and her lips. She could have ducked back behind Alec and let him shield her. But she was finished with that. It was time to face things head-on the only way she’d ever known—by herself. So she kept her arms out wide, leaned into the wind and let it dry the salty tears from her cheeks.

Chapter Twelve

When Zoey pushed through the circular door of the Northern Lights Inn the next morning, Anya and Clementine were already parked on barstools waiting for her at the coffee bar.

"Look at you two. I thought I was early." She shrugged out of her parka and glanced at her watch. She'd arrived for their coffee date with five minutes to spare. How was it possible she was the last one there?

Anya shifted seats, leaving the one between her and Clementine free for Zoey. "Your voice mail said you had a big announcement."

"The suspense is killing us. We've been here waiting for almost half an hour already." Clementine thrust a steaming mug of coffee toward her.

Zoey eyed it with suspicion. "How much sugar did you put in there?"

Clementine's sweet tooth was legendary. "Relax. Anya ordered for you and forbade me to touch it."

"You're welcome," Anya mouthed silently behind Clementine's back.

Zoey hid her grin behind the mug. "Thank you. Both of you."

She took a sip while Anya and Clementine watched her with mounting impatience.

"Now you're torturing us on purpose, aren't you?" Clementine crossed her arms.

"Come on. Spill the beans. What's your big news?" Anya asked.

"I'll give you a hint," Zoey said slyly and reached into her purse. She removed one of the Save the Reindeer donation jars and placed it on the counter.

"I don't get it." Clementine frowned.

Anya's brow furrowed. "Wait a minute. Just the other day you told me you weren't keeping any of the money you'd collected from those jars. So why are you putting them back out?"

"That was before," Zoey said.

"Before what?" Clementine asked.

Zoey's head spun as she thought back on all the events of the past two days—the thrill of seeing Palmer leap up and over the fence, the lump in her throat that refused to go away during her meeting at the lawyer's office and the way she couldn't make herself touch the pen when it was time to sign the sales agreement. But her most vivid memories were those involving Alec. If she closed her eyes she could still feel the wind on her face from their flight on his motorcycle. She could feel the warmth of his chest as she wrapped her arms around him for balance. And she could feel her heart skidding to a stop when he told her he'd found another job.

Before a lot of things... "Before I decided not to sell the reindeer after all."

"What?" Clementine plunked her coffee, with its towering mountain of whipped cream, on the counter.

"You're keeping them?" Anya asked. "*All* of them?"

"Every last one. I saw something the other night that changed everything—Palmer can fly."

Clementine frowned. “Flying reindeer? For real?”

“Not exactly. He jumped. Very high, though. He cleared the fence in the blink of an eye.” She couldn’t help but smile every time she thought about it. “I think…no, I *know*...that’s why Gus had them. And that’s why he left them to me.”

“Because you love to fly.” A slow smile came to Anya’s lips. “Wow.”

“I couldn’t go through with the sale. I just couldn’t.”

“But what about your airplane?” Clementine frowned as her gaze snagged on a ski plane landing on the frozen lake outside.

Zoey had situated herself so she faced away from the big picture window. Obviously, she couldn’t avoid the sight of planes landing and taking off forever. But she couldn’t quite bring herself to look. Not yet. “I had to cancel the deal.”

“You mean postpone, right?” Anya said.

“No. The seller wouldn’t give me any more time. The plane should be back on the market today, but I’m not giving up. I have a plan.” She prayed it would work. It had to.

Anya glanced at the reindeer mason jar. “More donation stations?”

“No. I don’t want to rely on charity. I thought we could kick the Save the Reindeer operation into high gear with a Christmas festival of sorts. What’s more Christmasy than reindeer, right? We could hold it right there on the reindeer farm on Christmas Eve. We could offer photos with the reindeer for five dollars each, hot chocolate for a dollar, maybe s’mores for two dollars? If I have a good turnout, I might be able to collect enough money to maintain the reindeer until next year and possibly even get my plane. So long as no one else buys it before then. What do you think?” She found herself holding her breath as she waited for their reaction. It had sounded like a brilliant plan when she’d concocted it in the middle of the night, but now she wasn’t so sure.

Clementine smiled. "It sounds like a great idea. Of course we'll help you. I can ask Ben to bring some of the dogs, and we can offer dog sledding. That should bring in a few dollars."

"I love it." Anya clapped her hands. "You can call it the Reindeer Roundup."

"Good. We have a plan." Zoey breathed a tentative sigh of relief. She would have her hands full throwing a Christmas festival together in less than two weeks, but what else did she have to do with her time? It wasn't as if she had a job at the moment.

And Alec would help, wouldn't he?

"So this is your big announcement?" Clementine almost looked disappointed.

"Yes."

Anya and Clementine exchanged a loaded glance.

No one said a word. Silence hovered over the coffee bar until Zoey could clearly make out the sound of another plane taking off on the runway behind the hotel.

She cleared her throat. Loudly. "I thought you guys might be more excited."

Anya reached out and squeezed her hand. "We're sorry. This just wasn't the news we were expecting."

"We thought your announcement would have something to do with Alec," Clementine said.

Zoey's throat tightened. "Why in the world would you think that?"

Clementine shrugged. "I don't know. I guess you two seem to have a special spark."

Zoey fought against the memory of resting her hand on Alec's chest and feeling the intense pounding of his heart beneath her fingertips. "What spark? There is no spark."

"If you say so," Anya muttered.

"I'm being serious. There's no spark. None whatsoever."

She slammed her coffee mug on the counter with a tad too much force. Coffee sloshed up and over the edge.

Clementine struggled to stifle a grin as she handed Zoey a napkin.

She took it and dabbed at the mess she'd made. Why did it seem as though all she did lately was make a mess of things? "It doesn't matter anyway because Alec doesn't work for me anymore. Rather, he won't once Christmas is over."

"What?" Clementine's jaw dropped.

"Are you serious?" Anya asked.

"Yes. He has a new job in Denali at the start of the New Year. He gave me his notice last night." *Under a sky filled with so much starlight it made me dizzy.*

"I don't understand. What are you going to do? You can't run the farm without him," Clementine said.

Zoey bristled. "Sure I can."

Anya shook her head. "Don't get me wrong. I know you're perfectly capable of taking care of yourself. You've proven that time and again. But think about this for a minute. You just gave up your airplane. You're planning to hold a giant fundraiser in less than two weeks. You have no job, a dwindling supply of money and a pasture full of reindeer that you know nothing about."

"Don't forget the dog," Clementine added.

"How could I forget?" Anya said. "You also have a furry dog that looks like a bear."

Zoey shrugged. "I know it sounds like a lot. But I can handle it." She totally could. Didn't Alec say he'd learned most of what he knew about the reindeer from Google? She knew how to use a computer, too. Problem solved.

But would Google know the perfect way to cheer her up after a bad day? Would Google take her flying? Would Google give her a dog?

She wrapped her hands around her steaming cup of coffee and tried not to compare it to the comforting warmth of Alec's huge leather jacket. "I'll be perfectly fine without Alec Wynn. You'll see."

Zoey stared into her mug so her friends wouldn't see the sadness that was surely visible in her eyes. Because, as much as she tried to convince herself otherwise, somewhere deep inside she wondered if she was in for a rather blue Christmas.

And an even bluer New Year.

Alec swung an ax over his head and brought it down on the block of wood in front of him with a powerful blow. He was rewarded with a resounding crack and the sight of two equal-sized logs rolling off the chopping block. He picked them up one at a time and threw them on the growing pile of firewood stacked next to Zoey's cabin.

Dasher ran a quick circle around the woodpile, nipping at the logs along the edge. Alec was pretty sure she was trying to herd them.

"Relax. They're not going anywhere," he said, wiping the perspiration from his brow.

He was sweating even though icicles nearly as long as his arms were hanging from the edge of the roof and a fresh layer of snow covered the ground. That had been the idea—get some exercise, work up a sweat and hopefully burn off some of the frustration eating away at his gut. He was definitely *not* out in this crazy weather chopping wood just to keep Zoey toasty warm in his absence.

She didn't need him to keep her warm. She didn't need him for anything. She'd made that perfectly clear.

He hauled another piece of wood onto the chopping block and split it in half with a single swing of the ax. He'd like to see Zoey try to do that. He was willing to bet she couldn't even pick up the ax.

His jaw clenched, and he tossed the logs onto the pile.

Why was he doing this? Certainly there were other ways to get some exercise, to let off steam. Zoey hadn't said a word to him since their motorcycle ride the night before. Why should he care if she had two sticks to rub together after he'd gone?

His head throbbed. On some level, he wondered if he was on the verge of losing it. Zoey's reaction to his news should have come as a relief. She hadn't gotten all emotional or asked him to reconsider the offer in Denali, like he'd thought she might. Not that he would have stayed if she'd asked. Zoey needed help. That much was certain. But he wasn't the man to take on that responsibility. If he stuck around, he'd only end up hurting her in the long run. He didn't know exactly how. Or when. But it was sure to happen. It was written in his DNA.

She would be better off without him.

He just hadn't realized she'd figured that out already.

"Stubborn female," he muttered and gave another block of wood a nice, solid whack with the ax.

Because that was what it really boiled down to—her insistence on doing everything on her own. It really wasn't about him. On a purely intellectual level, he knew as much. She didn't think she needed him because she didn't believe she needed anyone. Ever.

He wondered how much the deaths of her parents had to do with that belief. He also wondered where her God fit into the scheme of things. She was neck-deep in her church group, and he'd spotted her on more than one occasion sitting in the rocking chair on the porch in the early-morning hours wrapped in a pile of blankets with a Bible in her lap. Did she let God in? Or did she keep Him at arm's length like everyone else?

Alec shook his head. Who was he to question anyone's relationship with God? It wasn't as if he had things all figured out in that department. He'd only recently begun to pray again.

He took another whack at the wood. His shoulders were beginning to ache, and his arms felt loose, as if they could slip right out of their sockets. But his head was beginning to feel a bit clearer. Maybe by the time he plowed his way through an Alaskan winter's worth of firewood, he'd find something that vaguely resembled peace of mind.

He slipped his fleece layer over his head and added it to the heap of discarded clothing beside him. He was down to nothing more than old jeans and a T-shirt, but the bite of cold felt good against his bare arms. He inhaled a cooling lungful of mountain air then laughed as Dasher turned three circles and plopped down on his clothes with a contented sigh.

At least there was one female in his life who didn't drive him to the brink of crazy.

He drove the ax into the wood with a satisfying swing. Then, just as the ribbon of tension in his body had begun to unfurl, a truck pulled into the driveway. He easily spotted Zoey in the front passenger seat chatting away with the driver—a man whom Alec didn't recognize. And just in case the sight of her smiling and tossing her hair at a strange man wasn't enough to give him a migraine bigger than Alaska itself, behind the truck was a sleigh.

An actual sleigh.

Like something he might see at the North Pole.

He planted the head of the ax on the ground and leaned on the handle as he tried to catch his breath. From inside the truck, Zoey giggled. He could hear it clear across the yard. And it made his blood boil.

So much for his attempt to unwind. There wasn't enough wood in the entire arctic circle to release this kind of tension, even if he chopped it into toothpicks.

The stranger climbed down from the cab of the truck, unhooked the sleigh and then backed out of the drive as Zoey stood and waved a red-mittened hand at him. It took superhuman effort for Alec not to march over there and ask her where she'd been and why exactly there was something that resembled a prop from a Christmas pageant in the front yard. Yesterday, he might have done precisely that. But since they weren't exactly on speaking terms at the moment, he refrained.

Instead, he heaved the ax overhead and plowed into a chunk of wood. He hit it off-center this time, and a small piece flew up and nearly hit him in the head.

Perfect.

Zoey sprinted toward him, her blond hair flying in the wind. "Alec? Are you all right?"

Nothing like a near decapitation to break the ice.

"I'm fine," he muttered and took aim once again at the wood.

Chop!

"What are you doing?" She frowned at the woodpile.

What does it look like I'm doing? Making sure you don't freeze by Valentine's Day. "Getting some exercise. Nothing to worry about."

"I'm not worried." She rolled her eyes, then her emerald gaze seemed to snag on his biceps. Her cheeks flushed a pretty shade of pink. "Aren't you, um, cold?"

"I thought you weren't worried about me," he said, fighting off an accusatory grin.

She cleared her throat and dragged her gaze back to his. "Once again, I'm not. If you want to get frostbite, suit yourself."

Dasher chose that moment to climb off the pile of clothes and stretch her mouth in a wide yawn before scampering over to Zoey. Her tail wagged back and forth, sending snow flying in every direction as she threw herself into Zoey's legs.

"Well, hello there, gorgeous," Zoey cooed. "It's nice to see you, too."

For some reason, the sweet tone she used with the dog spiked Alec's frustration. He took another swing.

Chop!

"Where's Palmer?" she asked as one of the logs rolled off the chopping block and onto his toe.

What was going on? He'd never been so clumsy in his life. "He's napping. This one here wore him out." He gestured to Dasher, who was now on her back flailing in throes of delight as Zoey scratched her belly.

Zoey frowned at Alec's throbbing toe. "Maybe you should forget the firewood. There are easier ways to get exercise."

He tightened his grip on the ax. "I'm fine."

How many hours had he been out here, chopping away without incident? Then Zoey showed up and he turned into an awkward adolescent. It made him want to punch something. Or chop it in half.

She shook her head. "Whatever, Mr. Macho."

Maybe she was right. Perhaps he should forget the firewood and simply let her freeze.

He pointed the ax toward the sleigh, still sitting in the driveway as if Santa had parked it there after a hard day's work of letting kids sit in his lap at the local mall. "Were you going to mention what that thing is doing here, or were you thinking I hadn't noticed?"

She glanced over her shoulder. Her hair whipped around in the wind, reminding Alec what it had felt like to bury his fingers in those blond waves.

He clenched his fists.

She turned back around. "Oh, that. It's a sleigh."

"I know what a sleigh looks like. What's it doing here?" He could tell by the goofy smile on her face that he wasn't going to like her answer.

"It's part of the newest phase of my Save the Reindeer campaign." Her grin grew wider.

"Why do they need saving? You're keeping them." He peered around the corner of the barn. "And right now they're stuffing themselves with reindeer pellets. They look perfectly fine to me."

"They still cost money. And I'm still determined to buy an airplane. Hopefully, the Super Cub. So we're having a Christmas festival for the whole town. A fundraiser for the reindeer. It will be fun, don't you think?"

It was worse than he'd thought. "*We?* As in you and me?"

"Is that a problem?" Her lips curved into a frown, which did nothing to lessen their appeal.

How would he ever make it to Christmas?

Zoey had already stirred up a whole host of feelings inside him he'd rather not deal with, and now she wanted him to host a Christmas festival with her. "I'd say that was an understatement."

Her eyes grew wide, and she was wearing that nutty old-man hat again. The look was beginning to grow on Alec. "Why? You told me you were staying until Christmas. You promised."

She had him there. "I agreed to work for you until Christmas. I'm a ranch hand, not a party planner. Besides, I don't do Christmas."

She jammed her hands on her hips. "What does that mean?"

He wasn't about to launch into another explanation of his messed-up psyche. He had a right not to like Christmas. It wasn't a crime or anything.

"I told you—I don't go for all of that sappy Christmas stuff. Sorry. It's just not me." He shrugged and tried to ignore the fact that even Dasher appeared to be eyeing him with disdain.

"You're really determined to remain a Grinch for the rest of your life, aren't you?"

"I never said I was a Grinch."

"It was heavily implied." She narrowed her pretty green eyes as if she were waiting for him to slither down someone's chimney and steal their roast beast.

"I'll be happy to take care of any reindeer-related duties. You know that." And wasn't that Christmasy enough?

"I was hoping you'd say that." She smiled so wide, it frightened him a little. "Because I need you to teach a few of the reindeer how to pull the sleigh."

She was crazy. First off, there was no way he could harness-train a reindeer in less than two weeks. And second, no. Just no.

"By Christmas? Impossible." He crossed his arms. The ax handle fell on his still-throbbing toe. Naturally.

She stifled a grin and winked at him. "If anyone can do it, you can. I have faith in you, Ebenezer."

Chapter Thirteen

Zoey had a problem.

She had reindeer coming out of her ears, and she had a sleigh. And now she even had a Santa suit. It was spread out on the worktable of the thrift store in all its fuzzy red glory.

But Zoey was still short one Santa Claus.

"Santa is going to make an appearance at your reindeer festival, Zoey?" Pearl, the airport receptionist, had finally stopped by to select a few things for her new grandbaby. Her arms overflowed with onesies and knitted baby blankets.

"Yes, of course." Surely she wouldn't have to wear the suit herself. *Please, God, no.* "You should bring the new baby. We're taking Santa pictures."

"I wouldn't miss it. Everyone from the airport is coming." Pearl grinned and made her way back toward the baby aisle.

For a very brief, very desperate moment, Zoey considered asking Chuck Baker to wear the Santa suit...as if he had nothing better to do than play dress-up at her reindeer festival, and the air traffic would just take care of itself.

"I can't believe someone brought this in today, just in time for your big reindeer event. There are a few holes in it, but nothing I can't fix." Kirimi sent Zoey a reassuring wink and stuck a straight pin through the plush red suit, marking a tiny hole near the elbow.

Zoey picked up the fluffy white beard that went with the rest of the ensemble. Technically, it was closer to gray than white. Nothing that a good washing couldn't fix. "Where did this come from? Do you have any idea?"

Aurora had only recently gotten a department store, so it wasn't as though the town had a long history of department-store Santas.

"The youth pastor brought it by. I think it was used for a holiday outreach program a while back. It's in good condition, dear. Your festival will have a picture-perfect Santa." Kirimi held a few spools of red thread against the Santa suit. They all looked exactly the same to Zoey, but Kirimi chose one and winked. "Got it. The perfect red."

Picture-perfect Santa.

Of all people, why did those words bring Alec to mind? It was absurd. Alec was pretty much the anti-Santa.

She wanted him in the suit, though. She just couldn't help it. It seemed appropriate. He was the one who worked with the reindeer day in and day out. He was the one training them to pull the sleigh. He was the one who made her feel as though she wasn't in this all alone.

He's the one...

She blinked.

"Zoey, dear?" Kirimi planted her hands on her hips and stared at her expectantly. "I just asked you a question…three times. You're standing there staring at that fake white beard like it holds the secrets of the universe."

Such as why in the world I would ever think that Alec is the one? She tossed the beard back on the worktable. "Sorry. I got, um, distracted."

"Are you okay? I'm beginning to think you've bitten off more than you can chew with this whole Christmas festival."

"I'm fine." Other than the completely ludicrous thought that had hit her out of nowhere.

He's the one.

It was crazy. Of course he wasn't The One. She hated the thought of needing *any*one, much less *the* one. She was perfectly fine on her own. Besides, Alec had one foot out the door already.

Her heart clenched.

Kirimi eyed her with concern. "Forgive me, dear, but you don't look altogether fine."

"Gee, thanks."

"You know that's not what I meant. You're lovely as always. But you look a little sad." Kirimi slipped a reassuring arm around her.

"There's nothing to be sad about." Then why did she feel like crying sometimes? "Other than I don't have a Santa for the festival. I've got Rudolph covered. Thirty times over. But all those reindeer might be pulling an empty sleigh."

Kirimi unspooled a long strand of the red thread and snipped it with her scissors. "What about that nice young man who works for you? Alec, right? He seems like the logical choice."

"I can't ask him."

"Why in the world not? You're his boss, dear."

Zoey hesitated. People didn't just dislike Christmas on a whim. She knew Alec's feelings about the holiday were all tangled up with his childhood and his ex-fiancée, but she didn't feel right sharing that information. "It's complicated. I just can't."

Kirimi shrugged. "Well, I'm sure Brock will do it."

"Dress up as Santa? Really?"

"Sure. He loves dressing in crazy getups. You know that." Already finished repairing the first hole, she tied a knot in the thread and moved on to the next one.

"That's right. The bear suit." Zoey rolled her eyes. She'd forgotten Brock had been dressed as a grizzly bear the first time Anya had met him.

"I can ask him for you, if you like. He can't very well say no to his mother-in-law, can he?" Kirimi's kind brown face creased into a smile.

"I'll ask him. You're already doing so much to help."

"It's my pleasure, dear. You're every bit as much a daughter to me as Anya is." Kirimi's words hit Zoey square in the chest. Why was she so emotional lately? "Well, you've got a Santa. Now, what else is on your to-do list? You've only got a few days left to prepare."

"Well, Ben and Clementine are bringing one of their dog teams so the guests can go dog sledding. We're charging ten dollars for a ride around the farm." Dog sledding was always a huge attraction in Alaska. And Ben Grayson was a well-known professional musher, so Zoey had a feeling he'd have his work cut out for him. "And I've already got everything together for the antler wreath toss."

Kirimi glanced up from her work. "Antler wreath toss? I've never heard of such a thing."

Zoey laughed. "Alec found a whole stash of antlers that the reindeer shed a while back. I thought we could use them for a game. Kind of like horseshoes, only we'll toss wreaths onto antlers. We've got all those activities, plus a reindeer-petting area, where guests can interact with the reindeer and take photos. And then Santa and his sleigh will be the grand finale."

It sounded like a lot. But would it be enough?

Zoey folded and refolded the pants to the Santa suit. "Once I get the farm all decorated with Christmas lights and bring in some music, everything will be pretty much under control."

Except for the trivial matter of teaching the reindeer how to pull the sleigh.

But Alec had that covered.

At least she hoped he did.

I have faith in you, Ebenezer.

It was that line that had done him in. Not the Ebenezer part—that was just her inner princess messing with him. Again.

She'd told him she had faith in him. And she'd meant it. He could see it in her unwavering gaze, and it had just about turned his insides to mush.

She was completely misguided, of course. No one in his life had ever had any kind of faith in him. For good reason. What did he know about being a stand-up kind of guy?

He should have told her as much. He could have just said it. *You're wrong to have faith in me. I'll let you down. So for your own good, don't.*

But instead he'd just stood there and let her words sink into his soul.

I have faith in you.

And here he was, three days later, leading a reindeer by a rope around its neck, as though he were walking a dog. A very big dog. With pointy antlers.

"Come on, Prancer." He clipped the lead rope onto the reindeer's head harness. It pained him to call the poor thing Prancer. Her name was actually Gretchen, but Zoey had vetoed it on the grounds that it wasn't Christmasy enough. So she'd up and changed the animal's name.

Kind of like she'd changed his. She was still calling him Ebenezer. Alec pretended not to notice, figuring she'd go back to his real name once she realized her teasing was ineffective. So far she hadn't. He was almost impressed with her tenacity.

At least he'd managed to save Snowflake, Holly and Sparkle from being renamed. And Palmer. He'd put his foot down where Palmer was concerned. Zoey had reluctantly agreed.

It seemed the most mischievous reindeer of them all could do no wrong now that she knew he could "fly."

As Alec led Gretchen-now-Prancer to the sleigh, Brock's truck pulled into the drive.

Perfect timing.

Alec had asked Brock to come by and give him a hand with reindeer training for the day. Since they'd done so well with the halter and lead rope—and since the arrival of Christmas was becoming more imminent by the hour—Alec had decided it was time to hook them up to the sleigh. An extra pair of hands couldn't hurt.

What had seemed like a pretty good idea came into question when Brock stepped out of his truck. Alec might have been able to overlook the furry red-and-white Santa hat on Brock's head, but that was only the tip of the Jolly St. Nick iceberg. Brock was decked out in the whole getup—red suit, black boots, giant gold belt buckle. The only thing lacking was a pillow in the region of his stomach.

"Hey," Brock said as he approached. At least he hadn't said *ho, ho, ho.*

He was accompanied by a man Alec didn't recognize. The stranger rolled his eyes at Brock. "Don't you mean *ho, ho, ho?*"

And there it was. The first of what Alec assumed would be countless *ho, ho, ho* references. His temples throbbed. Maybe he should have just tried this on his own.

"Very funny." Brock grinned. Then he introduced his friend. "Alec, this is Ben Grayson. He mushes dogs, so I thought he might be able to help with your, ah, situation."

Alec shook Ben's hand. So now he had a situation. He thought about the state of things for a minute. He was surrounded by reindeer, Christmas was in a matter of days and Zoey was acting even nuttier than usual. Driving him even crazier than usual. A situation? Yeah, that sounded about right.

"It's Alec's fault I'm dressed this way." Brock gestured to his Santa suit.

"Is that so?" Ben coughed into his hand, a semisuccessful effort to hide the smirk on his face.

Alec frowned. "How do you figure?"

"Zoey needs a Santa for the sleigh. She wanted you, but she said you wouldn't do it."

"She never asked me." Not that he would have agreed, under any circumstances.

Still, she hadn't even asked.

He should have been relieved. Why wasn't he?

"That still doesn't explain why you're dressed as Santa *now.* The festival isn't for three days," Ben said.

"Dress rehearsal." Brock straightened his red furry hat.

There was no way Alec would have put that thing on his head. Not even for her. "Why don't we forget the suit and get started?"

"Sounds good," Ben said, still fighting a smirk.

Alec led them—and the reindeer he still had tethered with the lead rope—to the sleigh.

Ben looked it over. "This is a nice piece of equipment. Where did you say Zoey got it?"

Brock helped hold Prancer in place as Ben attempted to connect her harness to the sleigh. "She borrowed it from Tom Wilkins."

Finally. A name to go with the face. Alec looked up. "Who is this Tom Wilkins character, exactly?"

As soon as the words left his mouth, he was alarmed to realize that he sounded like an overprotective parent. Or worse, a jealous boyfriend.

It didn't go unnoticed.

Brock let out a laugh. "You're not jealous of Tom Wilkins, are you?"

"No," he sputtered, even though the sick feeling in the pit of his stomach felt an awful lot like jealousy.

What was happening to him? He shouldn't care about Tom Wilkins and his silly sleigh. He shouldn't care about anyone in Aurora. Least of all Zoey. He would be gone in a matter of days.

And yet…

And yet he couldn't help thinking about who might take his place once he was gone. With the farm, with the reindeer.

With Zoey.

If that weren't bad enough, somewhere in the periphery of his consciousness he was actually considering putting on the ridiculous Santa suit. He scarcely recognized himself.

"Yeah, you don't sound jealous at all." Brock's voice dripped with sarcasm.

Alec ground his teeth together.

"Relax." Ben gave Alec a slap on the back. "Tom Wilkins and Zoey went out a few times back in high school, but he's married with five kids now."

Five kids?

He felt better all of a sudden. "I really don't care."

Brock nodded slowly. "Sure you don't."

Even Ben, who'd known Alec for all of five minutes, looked as if he wasn't buying it. Alec was beginning to wonder if he bought it himself.

She deserves better than the likes of you.

He cleared his throat. "Shall we get back to the reindeer? I've got three days to figure this thing out."

"Sure. That's why we're here." Brock cast a knowing look in Ben's direction but let the matter drop. Thankfully.

Before long, they had four reindeer hooked up to the sleigh.

Prancer and Snowflake stood side by side in the lead position, with Holly and Sparkle directly behind.

"Do you think four will be enough?" The sleigh was big enough for only one or two people, and with inches upon inches of snow on the ground, it should slide easily. But Alec hated the idea of any of the reindeer getting hurt.

Ben nodded. "Four will be plenty. Actually, one reindeer could manage this sleigh."

Alec's gaze moved from Snowflake, pawing at the ground, to Ben. "You're kidding."

Ben ran a hand over Prancer's smooth side. "Nope. Reindeer are remarkably strong. And fortunately for you, extremely docile. They've been doing this kind of work for thousands of years, so it's in their blood. If you were trying this with just about any other animal, it would be another story entirely."

Alec supposed he should be grateful he'd landed on a farm with reindeer rather than moose or elk. Then again, if this were an elk farm, he wouldn't be neck-deep in jingle bells and glitter. "You know a lot about reindeer."

Ben shrugged. "Not really. I just know a lot about sledding."

"Well, they're hooked up, but they don't look like they're in much of a hurry to go anywhere," Brock said.

"With the kind of time frame you've got, I think the best idea is to keep using the lead rope and simply lead them where you want them to go with the sled. Will that work?" Ben cast a questioning glance in Alec's direction.

"Do I have a choice?"

Ben laughed. "Probably not."

"Then it'll work. Zoey just wants them to pull Santa around in the sleigh for a bit. And maybe give the children rides. She thinks the kids will get a kick out of it. I doubt anyone will notice if the reindeer need a little guidance." Alec picked up Prancer's and Snowflake's lead ropes and walked backward a few paces.

The reindeer fell in step with one another. The sleigh cut a clean path through the snow behind them. And even though it was a sight straight off the front of a Christmas card, Alec couldn't help the swell of joy that rose up in his chest. There was something special about seeing a group of magnificent reindeer pulling a sleigh. Even he could appreciate it.

Wait until Zoey sees this. She'll love it.

"Would you look at that?" Brock's huge grin was visible even beneath the puffy white cloud of his Santa beard. "They're doing it."

They're doing it, all right.

Ben let out a whoop of triumph and clapped his hands. "Gentlemen, it looks like the reindeer are ready for Christmas."

Alec's throat grew tight. He didn't say anything, for fear he might get choked up. Then he realized the fact that he was getting all misty over a bunch of reindeer and a sleigh was more of a cause for concern than what Ben and Brock might think.

What was happening to him?

Therefore, if anyone is in Christ, he is a new creation; the old has gone, the new has come.

The thought hit him out of the blue. He swayed on his feet from the force of it before dismissing it as fantasy. Hadn't he been fooled by such a notion before?

Impossible. No one can wave a magic wand and make the past disappear. Not me. Not Zoey. Not even God.

No matter how much he wished someone could.

Zoey reached a gloved hand into the huge box of Christmas lights she'd borrowed—another treasure someone had brought to the thrift shop—and tugged on one end of a green electrical cord. All the contents of the box lifted out at once in a giant wad of wires, bulbs and plugs.

"Would you look at this, Dasher? I think this tangle of cords is bigger than you are." Zoey dropped the mess back in the box, and the dog's ears pricked forward at the sound of her name.

She rose an inch off the porch, her furry body taut as a bow, ready to spring into action at Zoey's command.

"Relax. As capable as you are, I don't think untangling Christmas lights is your thing. That would require thumbs, which you don't have. No offense."

Dasher sighed, lowered herself back down on the braided rug in front of the threshold and rested her muzzle on her outstretched paws. She looked deceptively ordinary stretched out like that. Zoey knew better. Dasher always had one eye trained on Palmer. Even now, when both of the dog's eyelids were nearly closed, Zoey knew that if Palmer decided to stop scratching his chin on the fence post and mosey to the far end of the pasture, Dasher would spring to her feet before he took two steps.

Too bad she couldn't help with the lights. The dog's work ethic would have come in handy.

Zoey glanced up at the log columns and the slender log railing that wrapped around the length of the porch, imagining how great they'd looked wrapped in glittering lights. Like a winter wonderland. Perfect for the Reindeer Roundup.

She tossed her gloves aside. "I guess there's only one way to start."

She dug around until she found the end of one of the strands of lights and went to work systematically freeing it from the others. By the time she had three long strands of lights laid out in neat rows on the porch, her fingers had grown numb from the cold. But when she plugged the first string of lights into the outlet, her numb fingers were suddenly the least of her problems.

Nothing happened. No lights flickered to life. Not even the slightest twinkle.

Super.

Dasher's tail beat on the wooden floor of the porch in a gleeful tempo.

"What are you so happy about?" Zoey mumbled.

"Good morning to you, too."

Zoey's head snapped up. "Alec."

Great. Just what she needed. A Grinch. To make this experience even more pleasant.

She'd been so caught up in the lights that she hadn't even heard the rumble of his motorcycle. But he'd obviously been riding it, because his face was red, kissed by the wind, and his hair was charmingly rumpled. Helmet hair had never looked quite so good, which was patently unfair. Every time she'd worn his helmet she'd walked away looking like a drowned rat.

As usual, he was dressed head to toe in black. Snow dusted his shoulders, and he held two paper cups in his hands. The rich scents of peppermint and mocha swirled around him and made Zoey's mouth water.

His blue eyes narrowed. "Now I know something's wrong. You called me by my name instead of Ebenezer."

"I'm feeling rather Scroogy myself right now."

"Here. Maybe this will help." He handed her one of the mochas.

"Thank you." Her cheeks flushed.

He'd brought her coffee. *Good* coffee from the Northern Lights Inn. Since when did he do things like that?

Alec gazed quizzically at her cup as she brought it to her lips, as if he couldn't quite figure out the answer to that question himself.

He cleared his throat. “It’s some Christmas concoction. It sounded like something you’d enjoy. That was before I knew my Grinchiness had become contagious.”

“It’s not you. It’s that.” She waved a hand toward the box, still crammed with a pile of wires that resembled a tangle of green spaghetti. “I finally got a few strings of lights free, and they don’t even work.”

He fixed his gaze on the unlit strand and then back at her. Something in his cool blue eyes caused her stomach to tumble. “Would you like some help?”

He looked less than thrilled to make the offer. Was this some kind of test?

Zoey took a steadying inhale. “I thought you were a ranch hand, not a party planner.”

“I asked if you needed help.” Again, he didn’t sound all that eager to get tangled up in a bunch of Christmas lights.

“I can handle it.” She took another sip of the mocha and noticed a slight tremor in the cup.

Why were her hands shaking? Worse yet, why was there a flutter still deep in her belly?

“I didn’t ask if you could handle it. I asked if you wanted some help, which I would be happy to provide if you simply ask for it.” Finally, his lips quirked into a grin. A challenging grin, but a grin nonetheless.

“You want me to beg for your help?” No way. She’d rather untangle lights until her fingers froze and fell off.

“Not beg. Just ask.” He shrugged. He was the perfect picture of nonchalance.

It was infuriating.

Did he really think she couldn’t ask for help? That she couldn’t admit when she needed someone?

Not someone. Him.

Her cheeks grew hot as he stood there waiting. Now she’d have to ask for his help just to prove him wrong.

She lifted her chin defiantly. "Alec, my big strong rescuer…"

He shook his head. "No sarcasm."

"No sarcasm?"

"Nope."

She stared down at her cup. It was far easier than looking him in the eye. "Would you please help me, Alec?"

He reached out, gently cupped her chin and dragged her gaze to his. "Look at me, Zoey."

His voice was so unexpectedly tender, it cut straight to her heart. She felt tears gather at the backs of her eyes as she tried to form the words again. Why was this so difficult?

He's right. He's been right all along. I push people away because I don't want to need them.

It was a humbling realization. And more than a little terrifying. She didn't want to need anyone, least of all him.

"Alec." Her voice trembled. "Would you please help me?"

He smiled. It was probably the biggest smile she'd ever seen on that handsome face of his. "Of course, sweetheart. I thought you'd never ask."

The fluttering in her belly increased tenfold.

Good grief, what was wrong with her? He was helping her string Christmas lights…

…and calling her *sweetheart.* In a way that sounded oddly genuine.

He took a step closer. Zoey found herself growing light-headed, and she had to concentrate with all her might in order not to spill her mocha on his feet. He stood so close she could see the rise and fall of his impressive chest with each breath he took. She gave him a wobbly smile. At least, she thought it was a smile. She couldn't be sure since she'd suddenly lost all ability to focus on anything but his nearness.

He's not going to kiss me, is he?

She glanced at his mouth. Her heartbeat slammed into

overdrive as she realized she *wanted* him to kiss her. She wanted it very much.

He tilted his head and looked down at her with amusement dancing in his eyes. "Zoey," he said in a tone that positively smoldered.

"Yes?" she asked in a breathy whisper, her lips parting ever so slightly.

He pointed toward the ground. "You're standing on the Christmas lights."

She blinked. *What?*

"I'd love to give you a hand, but I can't so long as you're standing on the lights." Then—just in case her humiliation wasn't complete—he set his mocha down on the porch railing and picked her up by the shoulders, clear off her feet.

"Put me down!" she squealed. "What are you doing?"

"Helping." He chuckled. "Just like you asked."

"This is not helping. You're…you're manhandling me." And she'd thought he was going to kiss her. She was mortified.

He lowered her gently to the ground but left his hands firmly in place on her shoulders. "Calm down. This doesn't come any more naturally to me than it does to you, you know."

She scowled at him. "What are you talking about?"

His gaze softened, and his smile turned almost bittersweet. "You don't let yourself need anyone. And I don't let myself be needed."

She let her shoulders relax under the weight of his big hands. "Oh."

"Not to mention the fact that I'm basically living at Santa's workshop right now, and…"

"…and you're a Grinch."

"And I'm a Grinch." He rubbed her shoulders, and warmth began to blossom inside her. "I told you—I never grew up with any of this, Zoey. No twinkling lights, no sitting on Santa's lap, no presents under the tree. No tree, for that matter." His gaze darkened.

Zoey had to wonder if he was thinking about the Christmas when he'd almost had a tree…and a wife.

She still found it difficult to wrap her mind around the fact that Alec had once been engaged to be married. She just couldn't fathom it. And she was startled to realize she didn't *want* to imagine Alec with someone else.

"I'm sorry," she whispered.

"Sorry?"

"Yes. I'm sorry you grew up without those things, and I'm sorry about what happened with your fiancée. You're a good man, Alec. And she…"

"…got smart. She got smart. That's all." Alec nodded. *Firmly.*

The vulnerability slipped instantly from his expression. Before her eyes the thoughtful, sensitive man standing in front of her disappeared, leaving the old Alec in his place.

Zoey wanted to argue with him, but there was an edge to his posture that told her the discussion was closed. Permanently.

He removed his hands from her shoulders and crossed his arms in front of him. "I think we should get back to the lights now. Don't you?"

It wasn't a question. He bent to pick up the lights and scrutinize each bulb while Zoey could only stand and wonder about a little boy who'd never experienced Christmas. Who'd never believed in Santa Claus or sung a Christmas carol.

A man whose heart had been broken on Christmas Eve.

And as the furious wind whipped around them, bitter and cold, a little piece of her own heart broke, too.

Chapter Fourteen

Alec grimaced as he nudged his packed duffel bag with his foot, inching it closer to the door of his cabin. There it was—the sum total of his life, packed and folded into something smaller than a bag of reindeer feed. He'd always taken pride in the fact that he wasn't the type to cling to useless possessions, that he'd managed to build a satisfying life, free of unnecessary trappings and frills.

Now it just seemed pathetic. Like a cop-out of sorts.

What kind of person made it through thirty years of life with only a motorcycle and the clothes on his back to show for it?

The kind like your parents.

The kind like you.

He gave the duffel bag another scowl, kicked off his hiking boots and dropped down on the bed.

His mood had taken a dark turn in recent hours. He wished he could blame it on the tangled mess of Christmas lights he'd become intimately acquainted with over the course of the afternoon, but he knew better. As much as he would have liked to blame his bad temper on something—*anything*—to do with Christmas, he simply couldn't.

Because he'd almost enjoyed it. Particularly after he'd finally gotten Zoey to break down and admit she needed his help.

His lips curved into a smile just thinking about Zoey's indignation when he'd first demanded that she ask him nicely for assistance and how that stubborn fury had eventually melted away like a snowman on the first balmy day of spring. In that moment, something inside him had melted, as well. A warm sensation as real as the summer sun had passed through him as he'd watched her change of heart play out in her luminous green eyes. They'd gone from the color of a stormy sea to that of a field of clover in the span of a minute or two. He could see so much in those eyes of hers. Her fears, her secrets, her awareness of how very much he wanted to kiss her.

He'd miss those eyes. And the woman they belonged to.

Any satisfaction he'd gotten out of hearing her ask for his help, hearing her admit that she needed him, was tempered by the knowledge that it was a hollow victory. Tomorrow was Christmas Eve—the day of the Reindeer Roundup. The official last day of his tenure at the reindeer farm. Zoey might need him, but he'd be gone in less than forty-eight hours.

A soft knock sounded at the door. So quiet that at first he thought he'd only imagined it.

He frowned in the dim light of the cabin. That knock could only have come from one person. The one person he really didn't want to see right now.

Wasn't it enough that he was doing the right thing? He was sticking around to help with the Reindeer Roundup then leaving before things grew more complicated. Zoey might not be able to see it now, but life wouldn't always seem so cozy if he stayed at the farm. Sooner or later, he'd let her down. It was all he knew, all he'd ever known. Disappointment. Hurt. Pain. Even if he'd wanted to build something more with her—an admission he was in no way ready to make—he wouldn't know how.

As far as the genetic lottery went, he hadn't exactly won the jackpot. He was a marked man. Only time would tell what kind of darkness lurked deep inside him. If…*when*…it raised its ugly head, he wanted Zoey as far away as possible.

He cared about her far too much to stick around.

But that didn't mean leaving would be easy.

"Alec?" Zoey's voice drifted through the closed door. "It's me. Open up."

He pushed himself off the bed, slid his feet back into his shoes and opened the door just a crack. Barely wide enough for him to imagine he saw the glimmer of Christmas lights reflected in her eyes.

Those eyes.

"Zoey," he said flatly. "This isn't a good time."

She smiled as though he'd invited her in for Christmas dinner. "Come outside with me for a minute."

He shook his head. "Can't."

Can't? Or won't?

It didn't really matter. Spending time outside with Zoey in the moonlight fell under the category of very bad ideas. Everything about her—the lovely curve of her neck, her gentle smile, even the annoying way she typically crawled right under his skin—seemed magnified under the starry Alaskan sky. He had difficulty thinking straight with moonbeams caressing her porcelain skin, and he was beginning to question how long he could resist kissing her.

He might care about her enough to leave before he ended up hurting her, but he was only human.

"Yes, you can." She gave the door a poke with her pointer finger. "Come on. What can you possibly be doing that's so important?"

His mind drifted back to the duffel bag at his feet. "Packing."

She flinched a little.

Disappointment, he thought. *Get used to it.*

"You can spare a few minutes." She reached inside, circled slender fingers around his wrist and gave his arm a tug.

"Zoey, it's late. We have a big day tomorrow." He clamped his mouth shut when he realized it sounded like something a husband would say to a wife. *We have a big day tomorrow....*

Oblivious, her smile grew even bigger. "It's midnight. You know what that means, don't you?"

"That in six hours I have to feed a bunch of reindeer?" he said dryly.

She laughed. It sounded almost like the hopeful peal of church bells. "No, silly. It means it's officially Christmas Eve."

So this was about Christmas. Naturally.

"Zoey, you know I..."

She gave his arm another tug. A firm one this time. One that had him stumbling over the threshold and onto the porch.

"Surprise!" she said, her voice going quiet and taking on an almost shy quality.

She beamed up at him. As he expected, she looked even more beautiful than usual with subtle hints of frost and starlight in the thick waves of her blond hair. And for some reason, instead of her usual warm vanilla scent, she suddenly smelled of pine and freshly fallen snow.

Of Christmas.

He was bedazzled at first, knowing with absolute certainty that something significant was happening but so distracted by Zoey herself that he was unaware exactly what it was. Until she released her grip on his wrist, cupped his face with the gentlest of touches and turned his gaze so that it fell on the tree.

Right there on his front porch. A tree.

Covered from top to bottom in twinkling white lights, silver ribbons and delicate glass balls.

He switched his gaze back to Zoey. There were a million things he could have said, things he wanted to say. But his throat felt strangely tight all of a sudden, and he found himself incapable of uttering anything more than a single, disoriented syllable. "What?"

There was something astoundingly intimate about the way she looked at him then, almost as if she could see inside him. As though she understood him in a way no one else ever could. It reminded him of the way he'd once felt in God's presence. "Merry Christmas, Alec."

As Zoey watched Alec's emotions play out on his handsome face, she still wasn't quite sure if she'd done the right thing.

She'd known she was taking a risk. He'd never had a Christmas tree before, but that didn't necessarily mean he wanted one now. Maybe he thought it was too late. Maybe seeing it there would remind him of his former fiancée. The fiancée Zoey was having an increasingly difficult time thinking about. Not because she was jealous or anything. Because she wasn't.

She actually felt sorry for the woman, whoever she was. Had she really thought Alec would turn into some kind of monster? Zoey just couldn't see it. Alec might be a little rough around the edges, but underneath it all he was a wonderful man.

Too wonderful.

She swallowed around the lump in her throat as she watched the wonderful man in question reach out and touch the needles of the evergreen tree with a gentle brush of his fingertips.

Okay, so maybe she was just the slightest bit jealous.

She obviously cared for him. She'd figured out that much while tromping through the woods looking for a tree with a trunk small enough for her to chop down on her own. Beyond that, she didn't have a clue. Just what did she want from Alec Wynn?

Zoey's heart tripped. She had no idea what she was doing. There was no plan whatsoever. All she knew was that she'd wanted to rectify some of the wrong in his past, even if all she could do was this one tiny thing. She'd wanted to surprise him.

By the look of things, she'd done exactly that. He'd yet to utter a coherent sentence.

She wished he'd say something. She was beginning to feel as though this had been a big, sappy, sentimental mistake. Why would someone who did his best to ignore Christmas altogether want a tree anyway?

Alec raked a hand through his hair and took a step back from the tree. "Zoey…"

He didn't sound pleased. Then again, he didn't sound particularly annoyed, either. And she'd seen him annoyed on plenty of occasions.

"Do you like it?" She risked another glance at him, took a deep breath and held it as she waited for his response.

"Do I like it?" His gaze slid toward her, and the look of shock on his face slowly changed into something else entirely.

His mouth curved into a smile that could almost be described as giddy. Zoey couldn't help but think that he looked like a kid on Christmas morning. Seeing that expression of pure, unadulterated joy was so unexpected, so moving, that it caused a silent sob to well up in her chest. Her throat burned with the effort to keep her tears at bay. She didn't want anything to ruin the moment. Not tears. Not the fact that Alec was leaving so soon. Not anything.

"What is it, exactly?" There was a laugh on the heels of the question. A laugh unlike anything she'd ever heard from him before.

The sound of it skittered through her, squeezing her chest and making it difficult to breathe. "It's a Christmas tree, silly. *Your* Christmas tree."

His *first* Christmas tree. She found that thought wholly inconceivable.

"Yeah, I got that part." He laughed again, without a trace of his usual irony. Then he ran a thumb over the branch closest to him. "This is a real tree. Where did you get it?"

She shrugged. "Where trees usually come from. The woods."

"The woods?" His eyebrows shot to his hairline.

"Yes. This is Alaska, remember? You can't walk ten yards without tripping over an evergreen." She waved a hand toward the cluster of snowcapped greenery behind his little cabin.

"Please tell me you didn't chop this thing down all by yourself." His smile dimmed. Zoey had known it wouldn't last forever, but she'd hoped for more than a minute or two.

"Okay, I didn't." She crossed her arms.

Alec breathed out a relieved sigh. Some of the color that had drained from his face made a brief return.

She smiled. "Except that I sort of did."

"Zoey." Indignation crept back into his tone.

"Would you relax?" Why was she constantly having to tell him to relax, even after all this time? "You're not the only one who knows how to use an ax. It's a necessary skill for any Alaskan."

"So this is the sort of thing you're going to run around doing after I'm gone? Swinging a deadly weapon while you're alone in the woods? *At night?*" He looked down at her, the soft glow of the lights from the Christmas tree illuminating his chiseled cheekbones, his strong jaw. His lips.

For once, she didn't find his anger irritating. As much as she hated to admit it, it was actually sort of sweet. He was worried about her. He'd thought about what would happen to her once he'd left for Denali.

Something in her heart broke free. "Alec?"

He gave her a penetrating look but said nothing.

Her heart hammering into overdrive, she closed the short distance between them. "I don't want to talk about what's going to happen after you're gone. Not tonight."

The air between them grew very still while he considered her request. Zoey fixed her gaze on his cool blue eyes and watched as his irritation fell away and acceptance took its place. "Fair enough."

She stood so close to him that she felt his words rumble through her. She smiled. "Good."

"Good," he echoed, returning her smile.

She inhaled a tentative breath and the air around them began to move once more, crackling and humming with electricity. Something stirred inside her, as if she'd been lit from the inside out.

"Thank you for the tree." He reached for her hands and took them in his. "It might be the nicest thing anyone's ever done for me."

"You're welcome." How many things had he done without as a kid? Zoey didn't want to think about it.

But just then the tiny scar above his left eye, the one she'd been close enough to notice only once or twice before, caught the light coming off the Christmas tree. It glimmered in a pale, ghostly white slash right across his eyebrow. And for the first time she realized Alec hadn't gotten that scar from a childhood playground accident, a spill on a diving board or a fall from a tree house.

I come from a bad place.

How bad, exactly? Had Alec been abused?

She didn't want to believe it, but in her heart she knew it was true. It explained so much.

She let her gaze travel over his face, looking for more signs of his past, answers to the questions she'd had about him for so long now. There were no more scars. Not physical ones. But his eyes—the exact shade of gray-blue as the sea that churned against Alaska's shores—told another story. Alec still had plenty of scars, only they were deep inside where she couldn't see or touch them.

"The way you look at me sometimes…it gets me right here." Alec lifted their interlocked hands to his chest. "It's like you really see me."

"I do see you," she whispered.

So much had changed since that first day when he'd ridden up on his motorcycle in a swirl of snow, clad head to toe in black and sporting an Alaska-sized chip on his shoulder. She'd found him moody, temperamental and dangerous.

He'd reminded her of a superhero.

He still does.

She bit her lip as she released her hand from his and lifted it, slowly, gently toward his brow.

Alec's breath released in a single, sharp exhale. Undaunted, she ran her fingertips across his scar ever so slowly.

She fixed her gaze with his. "Is this…?"

She wasn't sure how to finish the question. But there was no need. Alec knew precisely what she was asking him.

He nodded slowly, the memory playing out in his eyes as they grew darker, stormier. "Yes. My father."

"When?" The pad of her thumb moved across his skin again in a tender, healing trail.

If only healing could come so easily.

"On my tenth birthday," he said, his voice going hoarse.

Zoey had spent the better part of her life believing that losing her parents was the most awful thing that could have happened to her. It was the pinnacle moment in her existence, a bold black line separating her life into two distinct categories—before and after. For years she'd labored under the misconception that this made her different in a way that other people would never understand. How could someone else know what it had been like…being left so completely and utterly alone?

Had she really been so naïve? There were worse things than losing both parents. Far worse. Alec's face bore the evidence.

She wanted to erase it. His scar. His hurt. His past. All of it.

She couldn't, of course. Such things weren't possible. The pain of Alec's past ran deep. It wasn't something she could simply kiss and make better.

But she could try.

She caught Alec's face in her hands, rose up onto the tips of her toes and closed her eyes. It was only a whisper of a kiss, the lightest possible brush of her lips against the cool white of his scar. But as her lips touched that place, the sole physical hint of all Alec had been through, she could feel the rapid beat of his pulse beneath her fingertips.

Before she could even think about opening her eyes, Alec circled both her wrists and removed her hands from his face. He let his forehead fall against hers. "Zoey."

There was a world of regret in the way he whispered her name.

She let her eyes drift open, knowing what she would find in his. Sure enough, there it was—the same guardedness, the same caution she always saw looking back at her. This time, though, it was tempered by a heavy dose of longing.

She studied his face. His jaw clenched, and suddenly a very different kind of tension played out in his features. A tension that betrayed what a struggle it was for him to keep the wall between them from crumbling down around their feet.

"Zoey," he said again, softer and more tenderly this time.

"I told you before that I come from a bad place. Worse than you can imagine."

"I know." She nodded and bored her gaze into his, wanting more than anything for him to understand how much truth her next words carried. "But that doesn't make you a bad man."

The words froze Alec on the spot. He became as still as stone. Snowflakes gathered in his eyelashes, and he didn't so much as blink.

Zoey swallowed back the tightness in her throat. *I've over-stepped. I've said something wrong.*

It needed to be said. She just didn't know if he was ready to hear it, least of all from her.

Help him believe it, God.

She let her gaze drift down to her wrists, still encircled in Alec's big hands. She wanted to touch his face while she still could, memorize every detail with her fingertips before it was too late. Before he left for good. But she didn't dare move. She'd already made what was beginning to feel like a huge mistake. There was no sense in humiliating herself further.

"Thank you." There was a wondrous timbre in his voice that sent Zoey's gaze flying back to his.

She found him staring down at her with undeniable fascination. And undeniable affection. Being the object of such a look filled her with a rush of warmth so at odds with the chill in the air that it shocked her.

Then his gaze fell on her mouth, and she forgot all about the weather, all about the Christmas tree, all about the thirty-one reindeer who were possibly spying on them at this very moment. She forgot everyone and everything but him.

He tightened his grip on her wrists and pulled her closer, until they were nearly nose to nose, until she could feel the pounding of his heart against her chest and she wasn't sure where her heartbeat stopped and his began. And in that final fleeting moment before he kissed her, he looked at her so purposefully she thought she would melt right there as snow flurries fluttered all around them.

Then his lips were on hers, and his hands moved to cradle her face, stroke her hair. A world of feelings swirled inside Zoey, from sheer exhilaration to a familiar awareness. She felt as though they'd kissed in another place and time long, long ago and had finally found their way back to each other.

"Merry Christmas," Alec whispered against her lips, and her soul breathed a long-overdue exhale.

"Merry Christmas," she answered breathlessly.

Then he pulled her closer still and kissed her again. There was an urgency in his kiss this time that she couldn't deny, which made her feel the coming loss of him deep in the center of her chest.

He pulled back to gaze down at her and run his fingertips along the side of her face.

"Alec, tomorrow..." she murmured.

"Shh. Not now, remember? Not tonight." He pressed a finger against her lips, still warm from his kisses. He smiled, but it was equal parts joyful and bittersweet. "Good night, sweetheart."

Then he released her, turned away and walked back inside his cabin. The door closed behind him with a soft but definite click, leaving her standing alone in the romantic glow of the lights from the Christmas tree.

She ran her hand over its branches, covered with a fine layer of powdery snow that sparkled like diamonds in the twinkling white lights. It was Christmas Eve in Alaska, and Alec had finally kissed her.

But what would tomorrow bring?

Good night, sweetheart.

Was it good night...or goodbye?

Chapter Fifteen

"Where's Alec?" Anya asked as she helped Zoey pass out paper cups of hot apple cider to the sizable crowd of people who were there for the Reindeer Roundup.

For the first time since Zoey had set foot on the farm, there were more people than reindeer on the property. She'd grown so accustomed to the peaceful stillness of her new home that it was almost unsettling to be part of the majority.

"I don't know exactly, but I'm sure he's around here somewhere," she said, stopping short of admitting to Anya that she hadn't actually seen Alec all morning.

It's not all that strange, she told herself. *There have been plenty of days when I haven't seen him until evening.*

And today was her big day. Anya and Clementine had shown up on her doorstep bright and early to help prepare for the festival. Time had flown by as they made last-minute arrangements, such as decorating the fence with swags of evergreen, wrapping red ribbons around the logs on the front porch of the cabin and gathering piles of antlers for the wreath toss.

If not for that kiss the night before, she probably wouldn't have even noticed that she hadn't seen him tending to the reindeer at one time or another. They'd been cared for—fed, groomed, even brushed for their big day. But somehow Alec had managed to do all of it without once crossing her path.

If not for that kiss...

Her heart stuttered at the memory of it. It had been some kiss. So why hadn't she seen Alec since?

"He's still in charge of the sleigh, right? Because it's almost time. Brock is already hiding out in the Santa suit so none of the kids see him." Anya glanced toward the house, "Santa's dressing room" as they'd jokingly begun to call it.

"Yes. I'm sure he has everything under control. I'm not worried a bit." And she wasn't worried—not about the reindeer or the sleigh.

Alec knew how important this day was to her. If everything went well, she might even earn enough money for the remainder of the down payment on her airplane. Her future was at stake.

She inhaled a ragged breath. *The future.*

The future was here now. All around her, people were snapping photos of the reindeer, sipping hot chocolate and sledding through the snow. This was her life. As much as she hated to think about it, she had the nagging suspicion that Alec was avoiding her just to prepare her for what would come after the Reindeer Roundup was over and he'd moved on. If so, she couldn't quite decide if he was being kind or cruel.

God, help me get through this. She swallowed. *I've finally learned that keeping people at arm's length won't prevent me from getting hurt. I wouldn't erase the past few weeks, even if I could, even if it meant I would never miss him. But I'm not quite ready for him to go.*

"Hey, you two." Clementine hustled toward them, both of her hands overflowing with antlers. "I've officially disbanded the antler ring toss. It's a cash cow, but it's getting a little out of control."

Zoey furrowed her brow. "How?"

"Some of the little boys decided that the antlers make good weapons. I just broke up a five-way sword fight. I figured no amount of money is worth someone getting their eye poked out." Clementine glanced down at the antlers in her hands and shook her head.

Zoey blinked. "They were fencing...with reindeer antlers?"

"Yep."

Anya snickered. "Only in Alaska."

"I think it might be time for Santa's sleigh to make its appearance, don't you?" Clementine asked.

Zoey glanced at her watch. "Yes. Actually, Brock should be warming up his *ho, ho, ho* right this minute."

Right on cue, "Santa Claus Is Coming to Town" started playing over the loudspeaker. Zoey, Anya and Clementine exchanged eager glances and headed to the fence for a better view.

The ring of jingle bells and the thunder of reindeer hooves preceded the actual arrival of Santa's sleigh. Before the sleigh even rounded the corner into view, everyone in attendance realized something special was happening. A cheer rose from the crowd as Alec rounded the corner, leading the team of reindeer that were all harnessed up to the sleigh. At least Zoey expected it to be Alec.

It wasn't. It was Brock, dressed in regular street clothes.

"Wait a minute. I thought Brock was supposed to be Santa," Clementine whispered, being careful so the children wouldn't overhear.

"He was. Alec was supposed to lead the reindeer pulling the sleigh." A tremor of fear passed through Zoey. *Where is he?*

The crowd started applauding, and toddlers climbed atop

their parents' shoulders for a better view. Everyone pressed toward the fence.

"What's going on?" Clementine stood on her tiptoes and craned her neck.

"I don't know. I can't see a thing. Surely we don't have a sleigh without a Santa Claus." But the moment the words left Zoey's mouth, a loud "ho, ho, ho" pierced the air.

She gasped, and a shiver ran down her spine.

"That's not Brock's voice." Anya frowned.

"No, it's not. It's Alec's," Zoey said, her throat clogging with emotion.

The voice that had become so familiar to her over the course of the past few weeks rang out, more exaggeratedly cheerful than she'd ever thought possible. "Ho, ho, ho! Merry Christmas!"

She shook her head in disbelief. "I've got to see this to believe it. Excuse me."

She wiggled her way through a mob of excited children until at last she reached the end of the fence closest to the barn where the sleigh was to be parked and Santa—*Alec*—would pose for photos with his reindeer. When she finally got her first glimpse, she simply stood there for a minute, frozen by what she saw.

Prancer, Holly, Snowflake and Sparkle were pulling the sleigh as if they'd been doing this sort of thing all their lives. Sleigh bells were strung all along their leather harnesses, jingling with each step the reindeer took, like something out of an old-fashioned Christmas carol.

Just hear those sleigh bells jingling, ring ting a tingling, too...

And sure enough, Alec sat atop the sleigh, dressed head to toe in full Santa Claus regalia. But that wasn't all. Dasher sat beside him, sporting a pair of felt reindeer antlers and a big red bow around her neck. It was just the kind of ridiculous getup that Alec most certainly considered beneath the dog's dignity, but he'd done it anyway.

For her.

She blinked back tears and fought the overwhelming urge to climb up into that sleigh and ride off into the Alaskan sunset with him. Or the North Pole. Wherever.

Because I'm in love with him.

Her breath caught in her throat. She couldn't be in love with Alec. She didn't want to be in love, especially not with someone she'd probably never see again after today.

From his perch at the top of the sleigh, Alec sought her out with his piercing blue gaze as he waved to the crowd. As silly as he looked in the comically fluffy white beard and furry red suit, he still somehow managed to take her breath away. And when at last he locked eyes with her, he winked, sending a zing of electricity straight to the center of her chest. To her heart.

Love. Most definitely.

A single, salty tear slipped down her cheek.

God, what am I supposed to do now?

Alec was still wearing his Jolly St. Nick garb hours after he'd passed out his last candy cane. Despite the fact that snow was falling so fast it was swallowing up the fence, the driveway, even the reindeer, he was hot. And itchy.

He had a whole new appreciation for department-store Santas. The uniform's comfort left much to be desired.

But it had all been worth it to see the look on Zoey's face when he rode in on that sleigh. He'd wanted to do something for her, something that would take her breath away. A perfect parting gift.

Mission accomplished. Only now, for some weird reason, he was reluctant to remove the crazy suit. So he left it on while he, Brock and Ben cleaned up the mess from the

Christmas festival. At least, he was supposed to be cleaning up. His attention kept drifting toward the windows of the cabin where he could occasionally spot Zoey, backlit by a cozy golden glow, chatting with her friends and counting the pile of dollar bills they'd collected over the course of the afternoon.

The two of them hadn't exchanged a single word since their kiss the night before, just a wink, a secret smile here and there, a handful of quiet looks while Christmas mayhem spun all around them. Perhaps it was for the best. What was left to say?

Besides goodbye.

"Apple cider?" Brock thrust a mug of fragrant, steaming liquid under Alec's nose.

"Thanks." Alec took the mug and glanced once more at the window, but Zoey had disappeared somewhere inside the cabin.

"Why don't you go on in, man?" Brock waved a gloved hand toward the house.

"Inside?" Alec turned his back to the cabin and the ribbon of smoke coming from its chimney that carried the warm scent of Christmas. Of home.

His throat tightened. "I don't think so."

"I see the way you look at her. And I'm the one you pried that ratty Santa suit off of earlier so you could surprise her, remember?" Brock crossed his arms and gave Alec's attire an amused once-over.

Why didn't he just take the crazy thing off? "And your point is?"

Brock pinned him with a look. "It's obvious you're head over heels in love with her. What are you waiting for? A sign from God?"

No. Yes. Maybe.

He was standing there dressed as Santa Claus. What further sign did he need?

Alec swallowed. "It's complicated."

"I can appreciate complicated. Believe me." Brock exhaled a frustrated sigh. His eyes darted once again to the cabin and then back to Alec.

Something was wrong. Alec could feel it.

He narrowed his gaze at Brock. "What aren't you saying?"

"It might be more complicated than you think."

I doubt it. "I'm not sure that's possible."

Brock shook his head. "She doesn't have enough."

"Enough what?" he asked, even though he had a sickening feeling he knew exactly what Brock was talking about.

"Money. Even after all this." Brock gestured toward the Christmas lights, the evergreen-trimmed fence and the sleigh, where a very sleepy Dasher was taking a well-deserved nap with phony antlers askew atop her furry head.

It couldn't be true. Things weren't supposed to end this way. Zoey was supposed to get everything she wanted, everything she deserved. The reindeer, her airplane and a man who was worthy of her love and affection.

His gut churned. "How do you know?"

Brock lowered his voice. "Anya told me, and she swore me to secrecy."

So Zoey wasn't even planning on telling him? Perfect. Just perfect.

"Look, I know this isn't your responsibility. Or your problem," Brock said.

"You're right. It's not," he ground out.

Then why did everything within him scream at him to fix it? To make things right, to give Zoey her happy ending.

To be that man who was worthy of her love and affection.

He lifted his gaze to the sky, where twilight was descending on the farm in dusky purples and grays.

Is this what You want, Lord? Or am I just looking for an excuse to stay?

He was a mess. He'd been a mess his whole life. Who was he to think he could do this?

I have faith in you, Ebenezer.

The words hit him with the force of an avalanche. And they seemed so silly under the circumstances that he almost laughed aloud. But he didn't.

Faith. Wasn't that what it all boiled down to?

He'd had faith once. And then he'd lost it, but being here… in *this* place, with *this* woman, he was beginning to find it again. Maybe, just maybe, faith would be enough.

He closed his eyes, and he saw the same thing he'd seen every time he closed his eyes since the night before—Zoey, his beautiful Zoey, looking up at him and telling him that just because he came from a bad place, it didn't mean he was a bad man.

She believed it down to her core.

Maybe it was time for him to believe it, too. To believe that whether or not he ended up like his parents wasn't a matter of genetics. It was a matter of choice. Not Zoey's choice to have faith in him, but his own choice to have faith in himself—and most of all, faith in God.

"Are you okay?" Brock's voice had a discernible note of concern.

At last, Alec opened his eyes. "Yeah. I think I actually might be all right." He let out a laugh.

"You sure about that?"

"I am, but I've got to go." He thrust his mug of cider at Brock and strode toward his motorcycle.

He was already straddling his bike and pulling on his helmet when Brock caught up with him. "You do realize you're still dressed as Santa Claus, right? Where are you going, anyway?"

Alec glanced down. He'd already forgotten about the Santa suit, but what difference did it make now? He looked back up at Brock as he cranked the engine of the motorcycle to life. "To make things right."

Zoey peeled back the red checkered curtain of the kitchen window and glanced again at the empty driveway.

Alec had been gone for hours. His motorcycle was no longer parked in its usual place, and no one seemed to have any idea where he'd gone. Even Brock claimed ignorance, which seemed odd because the two of them had been outside together all evening.

Not that she'd been spying on him out the window or anything.

Not much, anyway.

Taking an occasional peek at Alec was certainly more enjoyable than the scene that had played out around her kitchen table. Clementine and Anya had helped her organize the funds they'd raised at the festival, and even though nearly the entire population of Aurora had turned up to have photos taken with the reindeer and roast marshmallows over an open fire, she was still short for the down payment on her airplane. She'd done her best, and the people of Aurora had turned out in droves. But it still wasn't enough.

She'd been so sure she had things under control, and now everything was falling to pieces around her.

Anya, Brock, Clementine and Ben had stayed long after all the clean-up work was complete, sitting around the kitchen table and keeping her company. She'd finally shooed them all out the door when the clock neared midnight. It had been nice, though, having them rally around her, trying to keep her mind off the fact that she still didn't have enough money for her airplane.

No money. No plane. No job.

Her usual trifecta of problems.

But oddly enough, the thing that frightened her the most was the thought of no Alec. The rest she could handle. She wasn't exactly sure how, but she could deal with logistical details later. It was her heart she wasn't sure she could fix once they'd said their goodbyes.

If they said their goodbyes. Where was he, anyway?

She peered out the window again. Nothing. But as she replaced the curtain, a riot of frantic barks arose from the pasture. It was so loud and so sudden that Zoey jumped.

Dasher.

And then fear set in. *Palmer!* Not again.

She prayed as she shoved her arms into her parka and fumbled around in her pockets for her mittens. *Please, God, not again. I can't deal with this. Not now.*

Honestly, how much more could she take? It was Christmas Eve, and she very likely had a reindeer on the loose. She didn't even want to think about what kind of trouble Palmer could get into on a snowy night like this one. The weather outside bordered on blizzard conditions. He could get lost, permanently. Or worse, hit by a car.

The moment she opened the back door, she found herself on the receiving end of a face full of snow. It was coming down almost sideways in big, wet flakes. The pasture was nothing but a whirling white blur before her. If not for Dasher's panicked barks, she might not have even found it. She followed the commotion and managed to grab hold of the fence. A few steps later, she'd found the gate. She gave the latch a firm tug, but it slipped right through the damp palm of her mitten. She tried again to no avail. All the while Dasher barked and barked. Palmer was nowhere to be seen. She was sure he'd leaped over the fence again. Where had he gone this time? And how far had he gotten? Would Dasher even be able to catch up to him?

Fear coiled deep in her belly, and she wished, more than anything, that Alec was here.

But he wasn't. She might as well get used to the idea.

She pulled off her mittens and gave the latch a tug with her bare hand. Finally it gave way, and Dasher shot through the gate. Zoey barely hopped out of the dog's path in time to avoid being rammed right in the shins.

And then there was nothing but quiet.

The sudden stillness was eerie. Zoey sagged against the fence and peered into the snow-covered darkness, but she couldn't see a thing. Dasher was long gone, hot in pursuit of Palmer. Or so she hoped.

What if neither of them came back? Her throat grew thick. She wasn't sure she could take the loss of Alec, Palmer and Dasher all at once.

No more loss. Please, God.

Tears stung her eyes, and her face grew numb from the fierce wind and snow. She no longer knew if the pinpricks of cold on her cheeks were from the snowstorm or her own tears. She swiped at her face with one of her mittens, and for a fleeting moment, her vision cleared.

Something was coming toward her.

No, someone. A man.

Or was it?

Maybe she was hallucinating, because the blur of a person she saw approaching through a whirlwind of snow and sleet looked an awful lot like Santa Claus.

She wiped the snow from her eyes again. And everything in her world fell into place at the sight of Alec slowing to a stop before her with Dasher at his feet and Palmer's giant head looming over his shoulder.

Her gaze snagged on the Santa suit. Had he been wearing that thing all day? With snow crusting his eyelashes, his eyebrows and the dark stubble that always lined his perfectly square jaw, he even had a virtual white beard.

"Have you lost something?" he asked, grinning, frost gathering in the fine lines around his eyes.

Zoey suddenly had trouble finding her voice. "Yes." *So many things...*

He reached up and gave Palmer a pat on his broad muzzle. "I found these two on my way home."

On my way home. Zoey's heart swelled at his casual use of the term, even though she told herself not to put too much stock in it.

Home. The word glimmered inside her, like a star-swept sky.

"What's going on, Alec? You disappeared. And now here you are..." *Just in time.*

"I had some things to take care of. Why don't I get Palmer and Dasher tucked in for the night and then we can talk?" He reached out and brushed snow from her face with a gentle touch of his fingers. They were frigid. "Meet me inside?"

"Okay," she breathed.

But was everything okay?

Alec's hand had felt frigid against her skin. How long had he been out in this mess? And he seemed different somehow. She couldn't quite put her finger on it, but something had changed about him.

Don't be ridiculous. He's still Alec.

Zoey hurried inside, filled the teakettle with fresh water and threw another log on the fire in the hearth. She was jabbing at the burning embers with the poker when Alec walked up silently beside her. He slid his fingertips along the length of her arm and slipped the poker from her hands, taking over the task until a fresh, glowing flame blazed in the fireplace.

He glanced at her and smiled, the amber licks of the fire

casting a golden light over his chiseled features. Zoey almost felt as though she was seeing him for the first time.

He's such a beautiful man, inside and out.

Something was definitely different, though. Those were the same gray-blue eyes gazing down at her, but they were softer somehow. Less troubled.

He cleared his throat and reached for her hands. "Zoey..."

Was this it? Was this goodbye?

"Wait." She pulled her hands away. "Before you say anything, I have something for you."

Her hands trembled as she reached for the envelope on the coffee table. She'd told herself she would give it to him the first chance she had, before fear or pride or something equally pointless got in the way.

That still didn't make it any easier to actually hand it to him. On the outside, it was nothing more than a plain, brown envelope, but inside lay her heart.

"Here," she said, offering it to him with shaky fingers. "This is for you. Merry Christmas."

He gave it a quizzical look before slipping it from her hands. "Thank you, but what is this?"

"Open it."

He broke the seal and peered inside.

Zoey had to remind herself to breathe. She'd never felt so vulnerable in her life.

"Money?" He looked up at her, hurt clouding his eyes.

"The thousand dollars I owe you. Remember?"

Disgusted, he thrust the envelope back at her. "I don't want your money, Zoey."

She crossed her arms and refused to accept it. How was this going so horribly wrong? "There's more. Look inside."

He let out a groan of frustration and pulled out a sheet of paper folded into thirds. Zoey thought her heart might stop right then and there as he smoothed out the page and scanned the small black print that told him all the things she couldn't bring herself to say aloud.

"This is a deed." He held the paper very still, and his gaze flew back to her. "You're giving me half the reindeer farm? I don't understand."

"Not a gift. You've earned it. I could never have gotten through the past month without you. We're partners in this. You belong here, Alec. Please stay." There was so much more left to say, but her voice broke on the last word. She wrapped her arms around herself and stood waiting while he stared back down at the deed.

"It says here we'll be business partners. Is that what you want?" There was a sudden dangerous edge to his tone that made Zoey's stomach tumble.

"Yes." She nodded.

Yes, and so much more.

"I'm afraid I'm going to have to decline your offer." Then, to Zoey's horror, he tossed the deed on the fire. Its edges blackened and curled in a matter of seconds, turning her dreams to ash.

She could hardly believe what she was seeing. How had she read things so horribly wrong? She took a deep breath and leveled her gaze at him. "You don't want me to be your partner?"

Then, to her complete and utter astonishment, he dropped down on one knee and caught her hands in his. He pressed a gentle, reverent kiss to each one of her palms. "No, sweetheart. I want you to be my wife."

"Your wife?" She shook her head in disbelief. Surely she'd heard him wrong.

But there he was…on bended knee in a Santa suit, looking at her with such love in his eyes that it made her heart ache to the point of bursting.

"Really?" she asked breathlessly.

"Really. I'm in love with you, Zoey. I have been since that very first day, princess." He released a soft laugh. "I don't have a ring to give you. Not yet. But I do have this."

He reached inside the red jacket of the Santa suit and pulled out an envelope of his own. A slender red ribbon held it closed. "Here."

His eyes never left hers as she took it and pulled gently on the ribbon. The envelope fell open to reveal the last thing she'd ever expected to see inside.

"This is a bill of sale." She gave him a long, poignant look. "For my airplane."

"Just the down payment, but the monthly payments are very low. A handful of charter flights a month will cover it. We can make this work. I promise."

We.

Tears gathered at the backs of her eyes. "So you're staying?"

"I'm staying. You're right. My home is here. With you… you and all thirty-one of your reindeer," he said with a grin.

"What about Denali?"

"I called the park service this afternoon. They've offered me an alternate part-time position as a reindeer consultant. I'll have to travel there every three weeks or so, but I told them I know a charter pilot who might give me a lift." He winked at her, his eyes sparkling in the light of the fire.

She laughed. "I suppose that could be arranged."

Then she shook her head and looked back down at the bill of sale for the airplane. *Her* airplane. How was it possible? "How did you do this, Alec?"

"I sold my motorcycle. I seem to recall someone once telling me it wasn't the most practical method of transportation this close to the arctic circle." He shrugged as if what he'd done was of little importance.

He'd sacrificed his motorcycle.

Was that why he was half-covered in snow? How far had he walked?

A quiver of disbelief coursed through her. She lifted trembling fingers to her mouth as she did her best to absorb what he was saying. Alec loved her. He wanted to marry her. And he'd sold his motorcycle to make sure she got her plane. "I don't know what to say."

He rose to his feet, gathered her in his arms and whispered in her ear, "Say you love me. Say you'll marry me. Say yes."

Zoey's heart all but melted right there in the midst of an Alaskan snowstorm. A profound joy swelled inside her as Alec's words settled into her soul. He was in love with her. He would be her husband, and she would be his wife. Against all odds, they'd found each other. And at last they would both have the one thing that had been missing for so long—a family.

Thank You, God. Thank You.

She wound her arms around Alec's neck, pulled him closer and poured all her love, all her heart and soul, into a single, precious word. "Yes."

* * * * *

Dear Reader,

Christmas greetings from Aurora, Alaska!

Sleigh Bell Sweethearts is the third book in my Alaska series for Love Inspired. From the moment I started writing romances set in Alaska, I've been itching to write a Christmas story. Everything about Alaska's winter-wonderland setting lends itself to a snowy holiday romance—the goodwill and generosity of the Alaskan people, the acres and acres of evergreen trees, the beautiful snowcapped mountains and, of course, the reindeer!

In *Sleigh Bell Sweethearts,* Zoey Hathaway struggles to understand God's plan when she inherits a herd of reindeer. The antics of one naughty animal, in particular, along with her Grinch of a ranch hand, Alec Wynn, make her feel as though she's not up to the challenge of owning a reindeer farm. But as she and Alec work together to save the reindeer with Christmas looming on the horizon, Zoey begins to realize that every perfect gift is from above. Even the gifts that don't seem so perfect at first glance.

If you enjoyed Zoey and Alec's Alaskan romance, I hope you'll go back and read the first two books in this series, *Alaskan Hearts* and *Alaskan Hero.*

Merry Christmas to you and yours! May this holiday season be filled with all of God's peace and blessings.

Teri Wilson

Questions for Discussion

1. This story is a romance, but it is also about the importance of friendships and community. How do the various relationships in *Sleigh Bell Sweethearts* enhance the lives and faith of the main characters?

2. When Zoey first meets Alec, he comes across as surly and rude. Why do you think he acts this way? How do their first impressions of one another set the stage for the rest of the story?

3. This story centers around a reindeer farm. Before reading it, did you know much about reindeer? In what ways did the story surprise you about these animals?

4. In what way do the deaths of Zoey's parents color her view of the world? Have you experienced a loss such as this in your life? How did it change your beliefs about God?

5. Even though Zoey and Alec come from very different backgrounds, they are surprised to discover that they have a number of things in common. What similarities do they share?

6. How does Alec's previous experience with other Christians impact his relationship with the Lord? Do you think this is fair or unfair?

7. Do you think Alec did the right thing when he left home at seventeen years of age? Why or why not?

8. Have you ever felt the desire to have people see you in a new light? In what ways can leaving our past behind be both good and bad?

9. Why does Zoey have a difficult time with dating, and why do you think she's never had a meaningful relationship with a man?

10. Was the portrayal of Alaska in this story as you expected? Do you feel the Alaskan setting enhanced the romance between Zoey and Alec? Why or why not?

11. What role do the reindeer play in this story? Why do you think Zoey feels such a responsibility for thirty-one animals that she never even knew existed?

12. Why do you think Alec harbors such a dislike for Christmas?

13. Alec worries about how Zoey will manage living on the reindeer farm alone in his absence. What sort of unique challenges do you imagine she would have faced if the story had ended differently?

14. Why does Alec turn down Zoey's offer to be her business partner?

15. What are the central struggles that Zoey and Alec deal with in this book? In what ways do you identify with these characters?

SPECIAL EXCERPT FROM

Love Inspired

Bygones's intrepid reporter is on the trail of the town's mysterious benefactor. Will she succeed in her mission?

Read on for a preview of
COZY CHRISTMAS
by Valerie Hansen, the conclusion to
THE HEART OF MAIN STREET *series.*

Whitney Leigh rolled her eyes. "Romance! It's getting to be an epidemic."

Because she was alone in the car, she didn't try to temper her frustration. Fortunately, this time, the editor of the *Bygones Gazette* had assigned her to write a new series about the Save Our Streets project's six-month anniversary. If he had asked her for one more fluff piece on recent engagements, she would have screamed.

Parking in front of the Cozy Cup Café, she shivered and slid out.

As a lifelong citizen of Bygones, she was supposed to have been perfect for the job of ferreting out the hidden facts concerning the town's windfall. Too bad she had failed. Instead of an exposé, she'd ended up filling her column with news of people's love lives. But she was not going to quit investigating. No, sir. Not until she'd uncovered the real facts. Especially the name of their secret benefactor.

She stepped inside the Cozy Cup.

"What can I do for you?" Josh Smith asked.

Whitney was tempted to launch right into her real reason for being there. Instead, she merely said, "Fix me something warm?"

LIEXP1113

"Like what?"

"Surprise me."

She settled herself at one of the tables. There was something unique about this place. And, truth to tell, the same went for the other new businesses on Main. Each one had filled a need and become an integral part of Bygones in a mere five or six months.

Josh Smith was a prime example. He was what she considered young, yet he had quickly won over the older generations as well as the younger ones.

He stepped out from behind the counter with a steaming cup in one hand and a taller, whipped-cream-topped tumbler in the other.

"Your choice," he said pleasantly, placing both drinks on the table and joining her as if he already knew this was not a social call.

"I see you're not too busy this afternoon. Do you have time to talk?"

"I always have time for my favorite reporter," he said.

"How many reporters do you know?"

"Hmm, let's see." A widening grin made his eyes sparkle. "One."

Will Whitney get her story and find love in the process?

Pick up COZY CHRISTMAS to find out.
Available December 2013
wherever Love Inspired® Books are sold.

LIEXP1113